the playmaker

Cover Design by Emily Silver

Editing by Happily Editing Anns

www.authoremilysilver.com

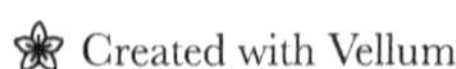 Created with Vellum

THE PLAYMAKER

A Nashville Knights Novel

EMILY SILVER

To all the found families out there that we love. We wouldn't be anywhere without them <3

Chapter One

BODE

It's the perfect day. Basking in the sunshine, with a cold beer in hand, there's worse ways to be spending a Saturday afternoon than hanging out at my pool.

Happy shouts from the kids splashing in the cool water echo around the yard. Most of my teammates and their families are here. Dax is playing with Marcus's kids, and Jasper is standing and talking with Noah and Graham while manning the grill.

"Will you play with us, Bode?" Sam asks.

A pair of goggles sits on her forehead, hair sticking to her face.

"What do you want to play?" I lean forward, dropping my feet in the water.

"How about chicken?"

"Chicken? What's that?"

If I'm using the pool, it's usually to stay in shape during the offseason. It's an easy way to get a workout in without having to go into the gym. I never actually play in it.

"We sit on your shoulders and try to push the other off." Sam looks at me like I should know this.

"Who would you be pushing off?" I ask.

"Sadie. She'll sit on Uncle Dax's shoulders."

"Is this safe?" I ask.

"What have we told you girls about playing this game?" Harper comes up from behind me, arms crossed with a fierce look on her face.

"Ahh, nuts," Sadie says. At least, I think it's Sadie. Honestly, it's hard to tell these two apart sometimes. Identical twins and all.

Sam gives a sigh. "That we're not allowed to play it because then Jamie will want to play and he's too little."

"Maybe after he goes down for a nap, okay?" Marcus comes up behind Harper and wraps his arms around her waist.

"Yes!" The twins pump their arms in unison as I hop up from the side of the pool. The girls start splashing Dax, who gives it right back to them. "Can we play with the big chess set after we swim?"

"Sure can," I tell them.

"You don't ever want this?" Marcus asks, nudging me in the side as I drop my sunglasses over my eyes.

"Fuck, no. Can you imagine me with a kid?"

Marcus laughs. "It's why we don't let you babysit the girls."

I shrug a shoulder. "I'd be offended if it weren't true."

"You'll want it one day," Harper says, without looking at me.

"Will I?" I quirk a brow at the two of them. The two of them were made to be parents. They're great at it. Me? I can't even manage uncle duty.

"I can't wait for the day when you'll eat your words."

"I don't think that day will ever come." I clap him on

the back. "Because I can do whatever the hell I want without anyone telling me what I can't do."

"Whatever you say, Bode. Whatever you say."

Marcus backs away from me as one of the kids does a cannonball into the pool. This is what I'm good at. Having my teammates over at my house and throwing a killer party? Yeah, this I can do.

Plus, with a few weeks off before offseason training starts, I might even go out tonight and see what kind of fun I can find with a willing partner.

The perfect day followed by an even better night.

Grabbing another beer from the cooler, I make my rounds, chatting with the guys who came. Some are here by themselves, while others came with their families.

The guys are sitting under the patio as I take one of the bratwursts and drop into one of the seats next to Marcus.

"Bode said we can play with his giant chess set when we're done," Sadie tells him. She's brimming with excitement. "And we're done."

"Are you sure, Bode?" Harper asks.

"Yeah. Who else is going to use it? I don't play chess."

"That's because I beat him."

Sadie has a huge smile on her face.

"That's mean, tiny Evans. I'll take you on after lunch."

"Twenty bucks says I win," Sadie says.

Marcus shakes his head. "Don't take that bet, Bode. You're going to lose."

I walk over and stick my hand out to her. "Oh no. I'll take you on."

"My sister is going to beat you," Sam pipes up.

"I always love watching Sadie kick your ass, Bode," Marcus says.

"You guys are mean, especially considering I invited everyone here."

"We like your pool," Noah deadpans.

"See if I ever invite you over again." I pull my sunglasses down and grab Noah's drink before heading back to the pool. But before I get far, a woman with a car seat carrier rounds the yard.

"Excuse me. Is there a Bode Adams here?" she asks.

"That's me." I hold out my hand for her to shake.

She glances at it and shifts what's in her arms. "I'm Miss Mitchell from the Tennessee Department of Children's Services."

A sound hits my ears. There's a tiny baby in the car seat that she's holding.

"Why are you here?" I ask, confused. "I don't have any kids."

I don't miss the whispers that Graham, Noah, and Jasper exchange.

"Oh, shit," Marcus whispers.

"I've been trying to get ahold of you for a few weeks now and was told you'd be here," the older woman says. She holds out a stack of papers to me, which I don't take. "This is your son."

"I'm sorry, what?" There's no way I could have heard her correctly.

"Your son."

"What the fuck?"

"If you would have answered any of my calls, you'd know who I am and why I'm here."

"Your calls? I haven't missed any calls."

"You have." Now she sounds exasperated. "It took me some time to track you down, but here. This is all the information regarding custody of the minor in question."

"Seriously, what the fuck is going on? This has to be a joke."

"Bode!" Marcus hisses. "You can't say that around a baby."

"He can't understand me," I snap.

The woman presses the papers into my hand as I glance at the kid that is now set on the ground. "If you would look at the paperwork here, you'll see that you are named as the baby's father."

My mouth is dry as sandpaper as I look at the information swirling together on the page. *A baby?* "There's no way this kid is mine."

"I am only here to relay the information provided to me. As you can see on the birth certificate, again, you were named the baby's father."

Her patience is wearing thin. Maybe because it's hot outside or because I have no idea what is going on, but damn it. What the *fuck* is going on?

The name of the mother doesn't ring a bell. I do my best to rack my brain, but I come up empty.

"And you're here because…"

"Because the mother is terminating her rights and wants the baby's father to have custody."

"How do I even know if this kid is mine?"

"Bode." Marcus elbows me in the side. "Look at him."

For the first time, I drop down and look at the kid inside the car seat.

Wide brown eyes.

Light-brown hair.

An almost-there dimple on his left cheek.

Fuck. The kid is a spitting image of me. Even I can see it.

"The mother was clear on giving custody to you, the

father. If you don't want him, I'm going to need you to sign some paperwork."

"For what?"

"Well, we would need to find another foster family for him to stay with and—"

Whatever else she says is drowned out by the echoing in my head. It feels like I'm underwater and gasping for breath.

I've never had an inkling of responsibility in the world. Just me and hockey. That's it.

Now, there's a baby on my doorstep.

"Can I have a minute?"

"I will need to know today. The family he's been staying with is going out of town, and we would need to line up another family."

"Right."

I glance at the baby before heading inside. I feel sick. The cool blast of air conditioning sticks to my overheated skin.

A baby?

Holy shit.

Of all the ways I thought today would go, this is not it.

"Bode? Are you okay?"

"What?"

I don't know who in the world is talking right now, but when I look up, the guys are surrounding me.

"I asked if you're okay," Jasper repeats. "You look like you're going to be sick."

"Here." Harper presses a bottle of water into my hand. "Drink that."

I chug it down in a few quick gulps. The coolness helps to clear some of the fog that has taken up residence in my head.

"Bode." Harper's clear voice cuts through the noise.

"You have to step up and do the right thing. This is your child. You can't let him go into the system."

I glance over at her. "Is that what would happen?"

She nods. "Yes. You can't let this sweet boy go with complete strangers."

"You know I'm a stranger to him, right?"

Jasper slaps me on the back of the head. "You're his father. Do you want to be a deadbeat dad, or are you gonna step up and be a man?"

"Fuck."

I scrub a hand over my face. Shit. That's the last thing I want.

I don't know the first thing about raising a kid, but after my childhood, do I want to be that guy? Damn it. Fucking Jasper knew exactly what to say to pull my head out of my ass.

"Okay."

"Okay, you're keeping him?" Harper asks.

"Okay, I'll keep him."

It's the scariest thing I'll ever say in my life.

Me? With a kid?

I have no idea what is going to happen, but I have to step up. I have to be this kid's father.

It's now or never.

I only hope this decision doesn't screw up both of our lives.

Chapter Two

BODE

"I just need a signature in a few places and then I'll be off."

That's it? A few signatures and this kid is mine?

That drowning feeling is back. I don't have the first idea on how to raise a kid. I take the pen from her hand and sign on each line she points to.

"I'll be checking in periodically, but since you are his father, this is an easy case."

"Okay?" It comes out more of a question.

"Here." Miss Mitchell takes a diaper bag and hands it over to me. "There are a few things in there that his foster family said he loves."

"Okay."

"My card is also here if you have any more questions." She eyes me for a moment before turning on her heel and leaving.

"That's it?" I shout after her.

"You're the baby's father. That's all there is to it."

Shit. I thought she'd be here for a while longer. She's not going to wait and let him get settled?

"Here's what we're going to do." Harper snaps into action. "Jasper, tell everyone to go home. Party's over. Marcus, we still have one of the cribs at home from the girls. Go home and bring it and any of Jamie's old baby clothes with you."

"I thought we were saving those just in case?" Marcus asks.

"Doesn't matter. Bode needs them more."

"Got it." Marcus pecks Harper on the cheek and is out the door.

"Now, Bode." Harper turns her attention on me. "You need to meet your son."

"Oh God."

I'm freaking out. Every cell in my body feels like it's on fire. Whatever happy, buzzy feelings I had earlier walked out the door when Miss Mitchell walked in with this kid, uh, I mean Caleb.

Harper pulls him out of his carrier and cradles him to her chest. He coos. Of course he does. Everyone loves her.

"Hi, sweetheart. Aren't you a little cutie?" Harper fusses over him as she walks him to me. "Are you ready to meet your dad?"

She passes him over to me, and I take him in my hands, not quite sure how to hold him. Caleb is eyeing me with contempt. Can a baby even look at someone like that? If they can, he definitely is.

"How old is he?" I ask. I don't know if I've ever held a baby before. Fuck. That makes me feel pathetic. I mean, I must have held Jamie at some point, right?

"The paperwork you just signed says seven months." Harper grabs my shoulders and steers me deeper into my living room, guiding me to sit on the couch. "You need to hold him against your chest."

"Uh, right."

Bringing him closer, he smells like a baby. Clean, like a soft powder. He gives me a gummy smile. At least he looks happy.

I'm trying to grab on to any memory of his mother, but I can't. The harder I try, the worse I feel.

God, I really am a dick. That's becoming more and more clear the longer I sit with him in my arms. But at least it's getting easier.

"Is he your baby?" one of Marcus's girls comes up to ask me.

"Sam, Sadie, why don't you go see if Jamie is awake, okay? Let's leave Bode alone right now."

"Okay." Their feet carry them toward the office as Harper drops down next to me.

"Is there anyone you want to call? Maybe they can come stay with you for a while?" Harper asks.

"Yeah," I groan.

"That doesn't sound like a good thing," Dax tells me.

"Because she's going to rip me a new one." I adjust Caleb in my arms and fish my phone out of my pocket. "Text Gran for me and let her know what's going on."

Knowing her, she'll be here within thirty minutes, breaking every speed limit to get here. Hearing she is a great-grandmother? Yeah, she'll be banging down the door within the hour.

"Are you ready to meet your great-grandma?" I ask Caleb.

He gnaws on his fist in response. I don't know how much time has passed since he was put in my arms, but he's happy. A smile sits on his face and fuck, he really is cute.

"Daddy's here!"

Marcus waltzes through the front door with parts of a

crib in his arms. Jasper and Dax are behind him, laden down with bags upon bags.

"I grabbed everything. I figured we can take what he doesn't need home with us."

"You're the best," Harper tells him.

It's then I notice a smell starting to infiltrate my senses. "Uhh, guys? He's making a face."

Harper smiles at me. "Marcus will show you how to change a diaper, and I'll have the guys start setting up his room."

"A diaper? Do we even have those?"

"Same day delivery!" Harper shouts behind her. "Everything you need will be here soon."

"C'mon, buddy. Time to get elbow deep in parenthood."

Marcus walks me through each step of what he does, and by the time he's peeling open the diaper, I think I'm going to be sick. Miss Mitchell had a pack of diapers she left. If only she'd left instructions on how to raise a baby.

"Oh my God." I gag. "How can something so small smell like this?"

Marcus laughs. Asshole. "Get used to it. Now, grab some wipes and clean him up."

I'm gentle as I wipe up the mess he made. My face is buried in my shoulder as I do my best not to get it on my hands. It's the most disgusting thing I'll ever do. I pull out wipe after wipe, dropping the used ones in the messy diaper.

"One will do."

"Excuse me if I've never done this before."

He shrugs. "You'll be doing it in your sleep in no time."

Marcus hands me the fresh diaper and I slide it under Caleb. Opening the tabs, I fasten it around him. "Is that good?"

Marcus nods. "Nice job. I'm going to go check on the guys, but deep breaths. You've got this. We're all here for you."

"Thanks."

I choke back the emotion that's clogging my throat. That's the first time anyone all day has said I can do this. It shouldn't mean as much to me as it does.

Whenever I make a decision, I jump in with both feet. It's how I've always lived my life. As soon as Harper told me he would go into the system, I made up my mind.

Honestly, I'm surprised people didn't try to talk me out of it because I'm not exactly the best father figure. Hell, I'm not even the best uncle material.

"Everyone out of the way." The front door bangs open, startling the baby in my arms. Great. More noise to add to the chaos of this day. This time, by someone much, *much* older than Caleb.

"Hi, Gran."

Fierce brown eyes bore into me. This is what I was expecting from her. "Don't you 'Hi, Gran' me, young man. You have a baby and you don't bother telling me?"

"Gran, you found out about an hour after me. It's not like I was hiding this from you."

She waves me off. Her short, cropped gray hair is tucked beneath a hat. Grabbing Caleb from my hold, she coos at him. "We will deal with your father later, you sweet boy. I'm your great-grandmother, but you can call me Gran."

"I don't think he can talk."

"Never mind you." Her fiery gaze snaps to mine. It's like night and day when she turns back to my son. *That's something that's going to take some getting used to.* "You are going to be so spoiled. I've always wanted a grandkid."

"And what am I?"

She ignores me while peppering his happy face with kisses. At least he's not screaming, so I have another thing to be thankful for.

"Hey Bode," Dax calls out from the bottom of the stairs. "You want to see his room?"

"Yes, we do," Gran answers for me.

I wave her in front of me and follow behind. Having raised her own child, and me, she's a natural at this. Caleb is staring at me as we walk up the stairs.

It's a look of fascination. One that I'm mirroring back at him. The only kids I've ever been around are Marcus's, and they're easy. Maybe I'll be lucky and get an easy kid too.

"I'll take him." Hitting the top step, I reach out to take Caleb from Gran. I need to get familiar with him, and…is it weird I want to be the one to show him his room?

Gran passes him over. "We're going to have a word later."

"I have no doubt." It'll be more than one word, but I figure the less sass I give her right now, the better.

Walking into the spare guest room, I find it completely transformed. "How in the world did you get this done?"

The crib is sitting in the corner with a mobile of animals hanging over it. The dresser now has what I'm assuming is a changing mat on top of it. The oversized chair by the window has a basket of books sitting next to it with a baby blanket thrown over it.

A complicated device—I think it's a baby monitor—is mounted in the corner of the room facing the crib.

"The guys helped. You'll need to figure out what to do with the furniture in the other room, but at least Caleb has his own space," Harper tells me.

This woman does not get enough credit. I know she directed the guys to do all of it. If she weren't here, I'd probably be cowering in the living room without a clue what to do.

"What do you think, buddy?" I ask Caleb. "Do you like it?"

His eyes stare at me, wide and wondering. He coos at me.

"I'll take that as a yes," Harper tells me. "I'll go get a bottle started for him. He'll need a nap, and then I can walk you through a few more things before we head out."

"Thank you, Harper. I mean it."

She presses up onto her toes and kisses my cheek. "We're here for you, Bode."

For the second time today, emotion is taking over. This has been the craziest day of my life. I keep waiting to wake up from this dream. Me with a baby? Kids were never in the cards for me. I didn't want them. Now, in the span of a few hours, my life has changed completely.

Dropping down into the chair, I hold Caleb in my lap as he stares up at me.

"I can do this, right?" I voice my concern to the only person who won't judge me, and the one person I don't want to fail.

Come hell or high water, I'll do whatever it takes for my son. To be a better dad than I ever had. It's a promise that I make to myself as much as him.

Because once I set my mind to something, I won't stop until I succeed.

"I promise, Caleb. No matter what happens, I'll be the best damn dad ever."

Chapter Three

STEVIE - ONE MONTH LATER

"Last chance, Stevie. Are you sure you don't want to stay with me?"

I sigh, shoving the key into my car and turning it a few times to get it to start. Great. Another thing to add to the never-ending to-do list. Get my car looked at.

"Thanks, Crestina, but I'm good."

"I hate that dick. I mean, he decides he no longer loves you and then has the gall to kick you out of the apartment? You're better off without him," she huffs.

"So you've told me."

It doesn't change the fact that my boyfriend came home two days ago, told me he didn't love me, and kicked me out of our shared apartment. Having to pack up my life, for what seems like the umpteenth time, was easy this time.

A few boxes and two suitcases? It wasn't hard.

"Listen, once you get settled at your grandma's, let's go out for drinks. I'm buying."

"I will hold you to that. Listen, I need to get going. Nan is expecting me."

"Tell her I said hi. Love you, babe."

"Love you."

I end the call and toss the phone into the front seat. I love my best friend, but living with her and her boyfriend when they just got engaged and I was unceremoniously dumped? No, thanks.

I'm already at rock bottom.

Well, whatever is below rock bottom.

I'll have to stay with Nan in her cottage apartment at a retirement center. As if getting kicked out by my boyfriend wasn't bad enough, now this?

The heat of the day presses in on me as I roll the windows down. Another thing that I need to fix, but don't have the money to deal with. Thankfully, Nan doesn't live far from me.

Turning into the main entrance, I pull my old junker of a car into an empty space and try not to cringe as the brakes squeal. Maybe saving some money by living with Nan will let me finally cross this item off my list.

Hopping out, I do my best to straighten my white, sleeveless blouse tucked into black jeans and go to her front door. There's a Christmas wreath hanging on the door with a Santa welcome mat. Odd choice considering it's well into summer.

Knocking on the door, I stand back and wait. And wait. No answer.

"Nan?" I knock again. "Are you in there?"

There's not a single sound inside.

Pulling my phone out of my pocket, I find her contact and tap on it. It rings once before it goes to voicemail.

Oh, she did not send me to voicemail.

Tapping again, it doesn't even ring before her cheery voicemail rings out.

"Hi, this is Deb. I'm not here. Leave a message, but make it good, because if not, I won't call you back."

"Nan. Where are you? You're not home and I need to drop everything off. I don't want to be driving around with everything in my car."

The blazing-hot Nashville sun is scorching my exposed shoulders.

Looking around, no one is outside. I can't blame people for wanting to stay inside. I love the sun, but even this is too much for me.

Spotting the main building, I tuck my keys into my front pocket and head that way. Maybe they know where my Nan is.

It's not like her to run off without telling me. I mean, she is the one to flit off to the casinos at the drop of a hat. But she always tells me where she's going. We're all we have left in the world.

Shoving open the glass door to the lobby, a wall of cool air greets me. Much better.

"Hi there. How can I help you today?" An older woman with cropped hair sits at the desk.

"I'm looking for Deb Campbell."

"Oh, are you her granddaughter?"

Her immediate recognition has dread settling in my gut. "Is everything okay?"

"Oh yes, she's fine. She asked me to give you this."

"What?" I grab the sheet of paper she holds out and open it. Her familiar scrawl is short and sweet.

Stevie,

Hi love. Eve and I have a new address.

If you're reading this, you probably already figured it out. I'll see you when you get here.

Xoxo
Nan

I STARE AT THE ADDRESS—COMPLETE with a security code for a gate—before stuffing it into my back pocket. What the hell? A note and an address?

"Has she been okay lately?" I ask the woman sitting behind the desk.

"Deb? Oh, she's been great. Although, she's gotten on some of the ladies' bad sides because she keeps winning at bridge."

I smile at that. Of course she has. I don't know how someone can have a knack for winning at bridge, but Nan does. Maybe that's where I get my skills. But I don't doubt she's on the bad side of all the players here.

Playing for candy bars is big stakes.

"I appreciate you passing this along." I hold up the note. "Did someone else move into her place?"

"They did."

I shake my head. "Of course. Thank you."

Now that I know she's fine, annoyance takes over. Heading outside, the heat takes my breath away.

She really couldn't have sent this via text? Or hell, I don't know, let me know she moved? Not exactly the way to find out your Nan is no longer living in the same place.

How am I the more responsible of the two of us?

My car door creaks as I open it and roll down the windows. I gave up on fixing the air in here a long time ago. Punching the address into my phone, I notice it's in one of the nicer parts of Nashville.

"What in the world is going on?" I say to myself. "Where did you go, Nan?"

Sweeping my hair into a high ponytail to keep it off my neck, I slide my sunglasses on. There's not the slightest sign of a breeze as I navigate late afternoon traffic.

This is one of the reasons I don't like living in Nashville. It seems no matter what time of day you're out, the roads are packed. Everyone is here to try and make it in the music scene, and that is not my cup of tea.

Hell, even if I had lofty ambitions, those would be taking a backseat right now. I need somewhere safe to lick my wounds after being dumped.

Except now, I have no idea where I'm going.

With each turn the GPS directs me, I'm driving past fancier and fancier houses. A far cry from the shabby downtown apartment I was living in. Coming to the neighborhood entrance, I type out the four-digit code on the paper and wait for the gates to open.

"Holy shit."

Each house sitting off the main road is massive. Red brick. Gray stone. A light sage hardwood. It's like each house is trying to show up the other. I'm pretty sure the one I just passed has a turret. If a witch flew out of there, I wouldn't be surprised.

I've never driven through any place so nice. When I'm told my destination will be on the left, my jaw drops.

Nan is living here?

Seriously, what in the world is going on? She goes from the tiny cottage at the retirement center to this?

It's practically a mansion. I have no idea the square footage as I turn my car onto the half-moon drive and park. The all-white house with a black roof looks modern, plucked right from the pages of a home renovation magazine. A porch leads to a set of natural wood front doors, with two large picture windows on the right, one on top of the other. To the left, there's a single door that matches the front, which looks like it could lead to an attached guest cottage of some kind. The landscaping is pristine—not a blade of grass out of place.

The front door opens, and finally I see a person I recognize.

"I thought I heard your car." Nan has her arms out, ready to welcome me in for a hug.

"Where are we and what am I doing here?"

"Now, now." She links her arm through mine when I don't return her hug. "It's too hot outside. Come in and we'll tell you what's going on."

As if that isn't ominous enough, a shrill cry rings out. "Is that…"

"A baby?" she interjects. "Yes. Stop dillydallying and get your rear inside."

"Okay, what in the world is going on?" My purse falls off my shoulder and onto the floor with a clatter.

Stepping inside, I'm immediately met by the most gorgeous set of brown eyes I've ever seen.

"Same question. What in the world is going on?"

Chapter Four

BODE

"Why won't he stop crying?" I plead to no one in particular.

I'm exhausted. It has been nothing but screaming and crying for the last week. Caleb has been with me for a month. Add in getting peed on this morning, and I'm ready for the day to be over.

It hasn't been the easiest month I've ever had, but I thought we were settling into a good routine.

That was what Harper drilled into my head. Routine. Babies thrive on routine.

Thank God it was the offseason because I don't think I'd be able to adjust to having a son during the regular season.

Which also causes new waves of panic to surface because I don't know how I'm going to make that work.

"I can see you're borrowing trouble," Gran tells me as she walks inside.

"What? No, I'm not."

Grabbing the half-empty coffee pot, she gets a mug from the cupboard and pours herself a cup. "Honey, I have raised you more than half your life. I see that face. You're worried."

"Why won't he stop crying?"

"Have you fed him?" Gran asks.

"Yes."

"Changed him?" She drops down onto a bar stool, kicking one leg over the other.

"Obviously."

Gran rolls her eyes at me. "Well, maybe he's just fussy. It happens with babies."

I sway Caleb in my arms. Tears wet his eyes as his bottom lip sticks out in a pout before he lets out a wail.

"Wait." He's flat-out screaming right now, but I think I've found the source of annoyance. "Is he getting teeth?"

"Let me see." Gran walks around the table and rubs a finger around in his mouth. "Oh, poor baby. He is cutting teeth."

"What do we do?"

Gran pats me on the shoulder and walks around to the freezer. "Let him chew on this."

She passes me a soft, squishy ring that is ice cold. Holding it up to Caleb, I wait for him to take it. His cries aren't as loud but he's not taking it. "C'mon, bud. It'll help."

A loud noise filters in from outside. Now what? Whatever it is causes Caleb to start screaming again.

"Oh, that must be Stevie." Deb flutters out of the kitchen.

"Stevie?" I question.

Stevie? Who the hell is this Stevie person? The last thing I need is another person in this house. I'm already at the limit.

"Oh, good." Gran leaves the kitchen, heading out to

the entryway. Following her, I now see there is a new woman standing there.

"Okay, what in the world is going on?"

My gaze flits between the two older women, who have guilty looks on their faces. "Same question. What in the world is going on?"

As if there's not enough people in my house, this woman walks in looking just as confused as I do. Although, her confused face is a hell of a lot sexier than mine.

Not that I need to be thinking about that.

Absolutely not.

"Bode William Adams. You do not speak to someone like that." Gran smacks the back of my head. "Stevie is a guest here."

"She said it first," I defend.

"Well, Stevie really isn't a guest," Deb corrects.

"Not a guest?" I question. Not only is Caleb still screaming, but a headache is starting to settle between my eyes. "You two need to tell me what is going on."

"Stevie is going to be staying with us for a while."

"She is?"

"I am?"

We question at the same time. Her blue eyes lock on to mine and damn. Even though she doesn't have the first clue what's going on, they're beautiful.

A blue like the sparkling night sky.

Two seconds in this woman's presence and I'm comparing her eyes to the night sky? What is wrong with me? I must be losing my mind.

An elbow to the side stirs my thoughts. "What?"

"I said Stevie is going to be staying with us while she gets back on her feet."

"And when did you run this by me?"

Gran crosses her arms and turns to me. "Since when do you kick people out of your house?"

"I'm not kicking anyone out. I'm just trying to figure out when I missed someone else moving in."

"Wait, you didn't know?" this Stevie woman asks me. "Nan. Are you serious?"

"You needed a place to stay and you were going to stay with me. It's only a slight change of address." Deb shrugs her shoulders like it's not a big deal.

I fight the groan. Clearly the two of us are in this together. When Gran moved in last month to help with Caleb, I didn't realize her best friend, Deb, was also a part of the deal. Something about how Gran needed a partner in crime to help her out.

I didn't realize helping out with Caleb required two sets of hands, but who was I to argue? I should have prodded deeper, because now, apparently, I'm getting another houseguest.

One that is much closer in age to me.

One that keeps drawing my eyes away from the troublemakers in question to her.

"Gran, can I talk to you for a minute?"

"I'll take Caleb." Deb takes the now calm baby from my arms.

"Thank you." Stalking toward the office, I wait for Gran to pass and close the door behind her. "Explain. Now."

"Deb's granddaughter needs a place to stay."

"I don't mean to be rude, but why did you offer my place without talking to me?"

"Because Stevie is going through a hard time and needs to stay with her Nan."

I sigh, pinching the bridge of my nose. "You realize I

have an eight-month-old, right? Do you think she really wants to stay with a baby who is now teething?"

Add that to my list of worries. Teething.

"And you have me and Deb here to help. You are going to go out and tell Stevie she is welcome here as long as she needs. We didn't kick you out, did we?"

Gran cocks an eyebrow at me as she pins me with a stare that says I should not mess with her. I hate that look. It's one I can't argue with, no matter how much I want to.

"You know this is my house, right?"

She shrugs a shoulder. "So? I would have gladly moved in here and kicked you to the curb to stay with that sweet baby boy of yours."

"Gee, thanks. Love you too."

Gran pats my cheek. "I know you do, and I love you more than you'll ever know. Now, go be the man I raised you to be and invite Stevie to stay with us."

I blow out a breath and do what she says. By the time we get back to the entryway, Caleb is gnawing on his ring as Stevie coos at him. Drool slides down his chin.

"He's cute," Stevie tells me.

"Thanks."

"Look, I can go," Stevie says. "You have a lot going on—"

"It's fine. You can stay here," I interject.

A hand brushes my back and I swear it's a warning shot from Gran. Fuck. I'm doing exactly what she asked. I'm being polite. It's not like she raised me in a barn. I can be polite. I'd flip her off…except that wouldn't be polite.

"I don't want to impose."

"C'mon. I'll show you to your room." I don't leave any time for response and start jogging up the stairs.

Probably for the best for me to lead the way. I don't

need to stare at her ass as I show her to her new living space.

"I'm going to apologize right now for my Nan," Stevie says. "I'm sorry she sprang this on you, and I'm sorry she's staying with you."

I snort a laugh. "She's just like my Gran, so it's really not that bad."

"They're two peas in a pod, aren't they?" Stevie smiles at me.

Damn. I really shouldn't like it as much as I do. It's soft and sweet and is doing funny things to my insides.

Get a grip, Bode. It's a fucking smile. You're not a teenager who has never seen a woman before.

"I'm sorry in advance." I sweep my arm out toward the only unoccupied room in the house. "I haven't been in here since I got Caleb."

"What?" She looks confused. "Since you got him?"

Two queen beds butt up against one another. A potted plant sits in the corner, and a box of knickknacks sits on the dresser. Books are stacked haphazardly on the desk chair that somehow ended up here.

"Story for another time. I'll work on getting all of this out of here today."

She shakes her head at me. "I can handle it. It's the least I can do."

"And have my Gran yell at me for making you do it? No."

"I'll be out of your hair before you can even move it," Stevie says. "I don't want to overstay my welcome."

"Take as long as you need."

"Are you sure?"

Stevie is standing in the middle of my guest room.

"It's fine. What's one more person in the house?"

"You won't even notice I'm here. I promise."

"Make yourself at home," I tell her.

It's better than what I actually want to say. Because I've already noticed her. And Stevie's presence in this house won't go unnoticed.

I shouldn't want her to stay. Stevie is a walking temptation. A sin I wouldn't mind repeating over and over again. But she's off-limits. The forbidden fruit.

Her best friend's granddaughter? Gran would castrate me if I tried anything with her. I'd like to keep my balls attached to my body.

Besides, I haven't been with another person since Caleb was dropped off at my doorstep.

I've been fine with that. My son is my only priority. Right up until this very moment, I was okay with it. I love Caleb. Even in these few short weeks, it's hard to imagine my life without him.

I would do anything for him.

It's a cruel twist of fate that the sexiest woman I've ever laid eyes on is now staying two doors down the hall from me.

Fuck. I really need to figure out a way to get this woman out of my head because otherwise, it's going to be a long few weeks.

Chapter Five

BODE

BODE

Tell me I'm being dramatic

JASPER

You're being dramatic

DAX

About what?

Is it wrong that I want to stay in my room
and hide out like a high schooler?

DAX

Are you really afraid of your grandma that
much?

No

JASPER

He totally is

NOAH

I mean, I am

NOAH

She'll take you down with a glare

It's not my grandma

GRAHAM

Then who is it?

Stevie

JASPER

Who is Stevie?

JASPER

Did we trade for a new player?

DAX

Yeah, we cut you last week

DAX

Didn't you hear?

Jasper

DAX

You're too easy

NOAH

Seriously though…did we get a new guy?

GRAHAM

No

GRAHAM

We would know

Stevie is Deb's granddaughter

My new roommate

MARCUS

Wait, did I miss something?

NOAH

We all missed something

Yeah, me too

Because now Deb's granddaughter is
staying with us

DAX

Oh shit

Yeah

MARCUS

Are you in trouble? Do you need to come
stay with us?

Would Harper let us?

MARCUS

I mean, she loves babies

MARCUS

So yes

I appreciate it

But I think I can handle her

JASPER

Can you?

Why couldn't I?

GRAHAM

The fact that you're texting us about it
raises a red flag

NOAH

I believe the exact words were hide out in
your room like a high schooler

I don't know why I bother with you idiots
sometimes

DAX

It's because you love us

MARCUS

And sometimes we give good advice

Sometimes...

MARCUS

Harper got you set up for Caleb

That was Harper, not you, Cap

MARCUS

She's my wife. It counts toward my good
deed points

MARCUS

Be a grownup and grow a pair

GRAHAM

Damn. That's some advice

JASPER

Advice I agree with

I can't wait to see your ugly mugs soon

MARCUS

Aww, you miss us

I miss hockey

I need to strap on some skates before I
forget how

DAX

We've got a cup to win, so you better not,
Playmaker

NOAH

Hey, he's not the only one that can make
plays

GRAHAM

Yeah, but when he sets you up, it's a thing
of beauty

GRAHAM

Sorry, babe

NOAH

It's a good thing you're cute

And now I'm going to go hide out because
you're getting mushy

NOAH

And here I thought you were growing in
expressing your feelings

So much for trying to feel better. Lately, whenever I need something, I text the guys. Ever since Caleb came into my life, if I need anything—no matter how big or small—they're there for me.

Except now.

Is it so wrong that I want to hide out in my room?

Not from any responsibility of life. No. I'm past that.

It's because of my new roommate.

Stevie.

Three days.

She's only been here three days, but already it's been three *long* days. Everywhere she goes in the house, her scent lingers. Like peaches and flowers. I can't pin it down, but every time she's near me, I'm wanting more of it.

Craving it.

Like I could survive off that alone.

Grabbing a T-shirt from my drawer, I throw it on and grab Caleb from his swing.

"I guess we can't hide out here all day." He giggles at me. "Are you going to be nice to Stevie? She's going to be here for a while, and we don't want to scare her off."

Caleb smiles up at me. I love seeing his smile. The one that looks like mine, right down to the slight quirk in the corner. Shutting my door behind me, I head downstairs but come to a dead stop.

Because the last thing I expect to see is staring me in the face.

Stevie. In a towel. In nothing but a towel.

Water sluices over her shoulders, and what I wouldn't give to be that water droplet disappearing beneath the towel.

Holy shit.

"Oh. Sorry." Stevie points to the door behind her. "I couldn't get the shower to work in my bathroom, so I used this one. I hope it's okay."

"Fine. Good. Yeah." Fuck. "It's fine. No problem at all." Caleb's happy squealing cuts the awkwardness. "Right. Need to feed him."

"Don't let me interrupt."

Stevie walks into her room and closes her door with a soft click.

Fuck. Fuck, fuck, fuck.

I really don't need to add images of Stevie in a towel to my mental torment. I barely know the woman who moved in down the hall, but I can't seem to stop thinking about her.

That's something new for me.

Settling Caleb into his high chair, I give him a toy to play with while I fix his breakfast. Sports news is playing softly in the background. With football season around the corner, it's mostly on which players are looking the best at training camp. I don't pay much attention. Until we start talking about which team is in the running to win the cup, I try to shut off that part of my brain.

Although, maybe it could be a good distraction right about now. Because no matter how hard I try, my mind keeps going back to the woman living in my guest room.

Her schedule and mine—well, Caleb's—clash. If Caleb is napping, you bet your ass I'm sleeping. If he's going to be up in the dead of night, I at least want to catch some z's when I can. No one tells you this when you have a kid.

Well, maybe they do, But no one would have told *me* because I didn't plan on having kids. I guess I'm learning as I go.

Glancing over my shoulder, a happy smile sits on Caleb's face as he watches me. Do parents ever get tired of looking at their kid and thinking how cute they are? Because Caleb is fucking adorable. I love that he looks like me. His light brown hair sticks out in every direction and, even when fussy, he never seems to be truly unhappy.

As far as kids go, I lucked out.

"Here you go, bud."

I set down the bowl of oatmeal and spoon on his high-chair tray, turning back to grab his bib so I can start feeding him.

Except we don't get that far. Because the warm food collides with my neck.

"Fuck me," I mutter.

I turn to look at Caleb, who is grinning from ear to ear. The bowl is upended, with a mess all over his high chair tray.

"Everything okay in here?"

Of course Stevie chooses this moment to walk in.

"Apparently not." Oatmeal drips down the back of my

neck. "You'd think I'd have learned by now not to leave things within arms' reach of Caleb that he could grab."

"And now it's all over you." Stevie smiles at me. "Let me help."

Stevie grabs a handful of paper towels and hands them to me before taking another one and wiping up Caleb's food.

"Thanks." I wipe the sticky oats off my neck, dropping the towels into the trash bin.

On top of needing to make another breakfast for Caleb, I'm going to have to shower and do another load of laundry now.

Why is that something no one ever tells you about kids? It's an endless cycle of laundry.

Lesson learned. Don't leave food in front of a baby.

"Mind if I grab a cup before I leave?" Stevie asks, pulling my attention back to her.

She really is stunning. Her blonde hair is swept up into a high ponytail. The pants she's wearing are doing nothing for her, but that black tank top? It clings to her every curve. Her shoulders? Who knew shoulders could be such a turn-on.

"Sure."

I grab the half-full pot and a fresh mug and pour her a cup, then start to make a new bowl of oatmeal for Caleb.

"Thanks."

"Where do you work?" I ask. It's about as interesting as asking about the weather, but I know nothing about this woman.

"I'm an aesthetician."

I blink at her. "Umm, what?"

She smiles. "I work at a spa. Southern Bliss? It's downtown, but I specialize in facials."

"Really? That's interesting."

Stevie winces as she sips on her coffee. "You don't have to pretend to be interested in it. Most aren't."

"I am. I've never met anyone that does it. Can't say I've ever gotten a facial."

She smiles at me. "Well, you have really good skin."

"And you'd know because you're the professional." I wink at her, causing a blush to creep up her cheeks.

"I should probably get going. I don't want to be late." She gulps down the rest of her hot drink. "And don't worry. I'll find a new place to live by the end of the week."

"You will? Why?"

"Look, I know you didn't sign up to have some random stranger stay with you and your son."

I point at her around my mug, leaning into the back of the counter. "Technically not a stranger. You're my grandma's friend's granddaughter."

That earns me a smile. "Well, I'm sure you don't want me around with your son."

"I honestly don't mind you staying." It's not a lie, but also, not quite the truth.

"Really?"

"It'd be nice to have another adult around here."

Stevie snickers. "What about our grandmas?"

I roll my eyes. "Well, ones that act like adults then. Someone more my age."

Even though having her here can be painful at times. A sexy woman that I have no right to be lusting after? Yeah, maybe I should let her leave. It'd be a hell of a lot easier on me.

"If you're sure…"

"I am."

Stevie breathes a sigh of relief. "I really do appreciate it. And look, if you need help with Caleb at all, I'm happy to help. I want to pay my share of rent too."

"You're not paying rent." I laugh. "My gran would rip me a new one if you paid me."

"So it's your house, but she rules the roost?"

I burst out laughing, accidentally knocking the spoon I was using the stir the oatmeal to the floor. Oatmeal splatters everywhere. I sigh. I guess no matter what I do, mealtime is always going to be a disaster.

"You could say that, yes."

"How about we don't tell them? I wouldn't feel right staying here without paying my way." Stevie rinses her mug out in the sink before hiding it away in the dishwasher. "It might not be much, but please let me."

There's an earnestness to her voice that I can't say no to. "Fine. But we don't tell them because I really don't want to be on the receiving end if they find out."

"Thank you. I'll pay you after work tonight."

"Take your time." It's not like I need the money for the house, but I'll take it if it makes her feel better."

"See you later."

"Bye," I call out after her. She's gone in the blink of an eye.

A laugh sounds from where Caleb is sitting. The look on his face is conniving, almost like he knows what I'm thinking when it comes to our latest houseguest.

"What is wrong with me? Get a grip, Bode," I chide myself.

I have more important things to worry about. Like my kid.

Stevie and whatever feelings I might have for her can go on the back burner.

Feelings? What feelings?

See? I can do it.

Chapter Six

"**K**nock, knock." I peek my head inside the pool house door. "Anyone home?"

"Stevie? What are you doing back here, sweetie?" Nan asks, popping up from the couch with more grace than someone her age should have.

"Bode took Caleb for a walk, so I thought I'd come see you."

"This is a nice surprise."

"I haven't seen you much since I moved in."

More like I needed to get away from Bode. Away from the scent of his cologne. Or bodywash? I can't tell, but being around him makes things tingle that haven't tingled in a long time.

Is it because of that swoopy hair that flops across his forehead? That perfect jaw line that always seems to have the right amount of scruff? Or those deep brown eyes that lock on to mine when I walk into a room?

I don't need to be around another man like Bode right now. I don't know him as far as I can throw him, but a man that good-looking can only be trouble.

"How about a glass of wine?" Nan smiles at me as she walks into the kitchen and grabs a bottle from the fridge.

"Sure."

"I have your favorite rosé." She winks at me.

"Thanks." I look around the open floor plan of the pool house. "I'd definitely say you upgraded your digs, Nan."

"Pool house, my ass. I don't see a single thing in here to fix a pool," Nan tells me, shaking her head and handing over a glass filled to the brim with pink liquid.

"Pretty sure you could fit all of my apartments in here and have room to spare."

Wooden shutters are drawn over the French doors, hiding the living room and kitchen from the main house. A set of stairs at the back of the room leads up to the bedrooms.

Everything in here is cozy. It looks lived-in. Not that Bode's place doesn't, but his vibe feels more modern to me.

This? This looks exactly like how my Nan would live.

"Are you settling in?" Nan pats the space on the couch next to her and I take a seat.

"For the most part." I nod, sipping on the cool, fruity wine. It's needed after sorting through my pathetic box of things next door. "I don't plan on being here that long."

"Why not?"

"Because I don't want to intrude. And Bode is basically a stranger."

"A hot stranger," Nan corrects.

"You cannot say that!" I sputter.

"What part of that statement is not true?" She quirks a brow at me.

I sigh, running my fingertip along the rim of my glass. She's not wrong. Bode Adams? A man that sexy is trouble.

The kind that is so effortlessly sexy, he doesn't even have to try.

That kind of trouble isn't worth it.

Well, maybe a little.

But not right now. I don't need to focus on him. I only want to focus on me and getting back on my feet.

"I know that face." Nan startles me out of my thoughts.

"What face? I'm not making any sort of face."

"You think I don't know what that means?" Nan asks. "You're thinking about Bode."

I gulp down more wine than is necessary and end up choking around it. Shit. Way to not give myself up to the one person who can read me like an open book.

"Getting involved with Bode is the last thing I need right now."

Want? Absolutely.

"You worry too much about things," Nan tells me.

"Me? How can I not worry when I don't have a place to live?"

"You do have a place to live," she corrects.

"You know what I mean."

She waves me off. "That Brady was an asshole to you. I don't know what you ever saw in him."

I snort around the sip I just took, wiping my mouth. "Nan. When have you ever liked anyone I dated?"

"That Mikey was nice."

I roll my eyes and mop up the wine on the edge of my glass with my sleeve. "That was in seventh grade. You've really never liked anyone since then?"

"Well, maybe when you date someone worth liking, I'll like them. Like Bode."

"And how well do you actually know Bode, hmm?" I

tuck my legs under my butt and cozy up into the couch cushions.

"Only what I know from Eve."

"He's a player, Nan."

I looked him up. It wasn't hard to find Bode Adams. After a brief tour of the house, and a few words from Nan, I learned all I needed to about my landlord.

Bode has played for the Nashville Knights since he was drafted out of college. He's one of the top players for the team, which has seen a resurgence from one of the worst teams in the league to being a contender.

I know a few things about sports, but not much.

What I did notice? The ad campaign Bode did for a sports drink. Why they need to show so much skin to sell a sports drink is not for me to decide.

But with abs like that? No wonder Bode has a reputation.

Something I also discovered in my searching.

"If he's such a player, then how come I've never seen him with another woman?"

"I…well, how would I know? I just moved in."

"Stephanie, Stevie, darling," Nan starts, "I love you more than anyone in this world, but you take life too seriously."

I'm back to fiddling with the rim of my wine glass. "How can I not?"

In my twenty-five years, it seems like nothing has ever gone right. Maybe I'm looking in all the wrong places, but between men, apartments, and making ends meet, it always seems like I'm moving away from where I want to be in life.

"You were never dealt the best hand, but that doesn't mean you have to bear that weight every day. You can hang it up and let go every once in a while."

"How can I trust myself?" I voice my deepest fear to the one person who I know won't judge me for it. "Every time I think I'm making the right decision, it blows up in my face."

"Sweetheart." Nan pats my cheek. "I'm not saying you need to jump into any kind of relationship with anyone. But if you go looking for the worst in people, you'll always find it."

I blow out a breath. "Sometimes what you say makes sense."

"I can be smart when I want to be." She taps her temple. "Now, let's watch some baking shows and wish we could bake."

"Hey. I know how to bake, thank you very much."

"Well, then maybe you need to have a lesson for everyone in the house."

All I can do is laugh. Being around my grandma makes this weird in-between phase better. Before, I've always had my own place. If things went sideways with a guy, I had my sanctuary. Things like where I was going to spend the night was never a problem.

I went against my better judgment and got swept up in a pair of pretty green eyes. Move in after a month? Why not?

Maybe getting kicked out and ending up with Nan is where I'm meant to be in this stage of life. Focusing on myself and my job.

If I can hold on to that for a little while longer, everything will be okay.

And maybe this time, a pair of mesmerizing brown eyes won't distract me from my plans.

Chapter Seven

BODE

"**M**r. Adams. How are you doing?" our security guard calls out to me.

"Hey, Ronny. I'm good. How are you?"

"Just fine, just fine. Ready for the season to start."

"You and me both." I clap him on the shoulder as he buzzes open the door to the players' entrance.

Taking a deep breath, the familiar scent welcomes me home. The one that's hard to describe, but is the exact same in every arena.

That cold and sweaty smell. The hopes and dreams of hockey.

It invigorates me as I walk down the cement hall toward the locker room for our first day of offseason practice.

When I woke up this morning, I was buzzing. It's something I always feel before the start of a new season. That promise of something new. A fresh start. It's my favorite thing in the world.

The sound of music leads me toward the locker room,

pulling a smile from me. It's not a song I'm familiar with, but walking into the locker room, I see the guys.

Wooden lockers are lit from above. Red carpet covers the floor. The Knights logo hangs on the back wall, like a beacon welcoming me home.

This has always been the one place I felt at home. The one thing I'm good at. Before, hockey was always the one thing in life I had that I could depend on.

Now, I have more in life.

A son to think about.

"Hey, Bode." Marcus claps me on the shoulder as I drop my bag down onto the bench seat. "How are things going?"

"You mean since the last time I texted you guys?"

"You do text a lot," Dax says, coming up behind me.

"A lot can change in a few days," Marcus says.

I shake my head. "Hell, even a few hours."

Pulling a few things out, I see my jersey hanging in my locker. The number nineteen is there in big white print. The Knights logo sits just below the collar. I finger the thick fabric of my name on the back.

Somehow, starting this season feels different. I'm excited, don't get me wrong. I'm years into this career, and for the first time, it feels like I'm playing for something bigger than myself.

I don't want to be *that guy* anymore. The one that shows up to a bar looking for women. I feel so far removed from that guy, it's not even funny.

"Gentlemen." Coach Andrews's voice calls everyone to attention. "Are you ready for a new season?"

Shouts and cheers ring out in the locker room.

"Good, good. I've got big plans for this team. We had a deep playoff run last year, and I want to continue that success. Continue moving this team forward. The Knights have put together a talented team, and I'm excited to see where we go as one."

There's an electricity pulsing through the group of guys in the locker room. I'm buzzing again. I've never been so antsy for a season to start. Before, I loved the offseason, spending my time with different women and basking in the attention.

The only attention I want now is from the one person who seems to be just fine with no attention at all.

Stevie.

It seems no matter what I do, our schedules never sync up. The woman staying in my house is a stranger to me. I might know what she does, but that's about it.

One thing I do know is that she is stunning.

Shaking the stupor this woman continuously pulls me into, I change into my gear and grab my stick to hit the ice.

Taking a deep breath, I relish the smell of the ice. The cold seeps into me and reminds me that I'm home.

This is where I excel. Playing hockey. No matter what else is going on in my life, I can push all of that out of my head for a few hours and focus on my game.

That's what the team deserves. I know Caleb is in good hands with Gran. I think she mentioned taking him on a walk to the park.

"We're going to do line drills," Coach Andrews bellows. Everyone groans. "No complaining. We're going to build the endurance in your legs. My goal is to make it to the finals this season. I don't want us losing because your conditioning isn't up to the challenge."

All the guys gather on the line by the goal. When the whistle blows, we skate to the blue line, then back. Center line and back. We do it for every line on the ice.

I fucking hate these drills. They were designed by a sadist to make us hate hockey. By the time Coach blows the whistle, dismissing us to work with our line coaches, my legs are screaming at me.

My thighs are on fire as I skate to the bench to grab a few swigs of water.

Our coach starts running us through some different drills with the new guys on the team. A few we traded for I recognize from playing, but I'm not familiar with any of the rookies.

Marcus is already chatting with them. Knowing him, he studied up on all of them since he's our captain. It would be something he would do.

Before I know it, Coach Andrews is calling us all back to center ice.

"For this last part of practice, we're going to be doing something a little different."

The guys are huffing and puffing. Our chests are heaving after doing that last round of drills.

"What is it, Coach?" Marcus asks, ever the captain.

"Something fun. Three on three handball." The assistant coaches are lining up the goals on both ends of the ice. "We're going to be splitting into teams of three. You can't hold on to the ball for more than three seconds or the other team gets the ball. First team to twenty-one gets out of line drills tomorrow."

"Hell, yeah!" I shout.

"Coach, how is this helping?" Dax asks.

"It'll help with your edgework, balance, and even spatial awareness. Knowing where the guys are on the ice for your team. With new teammates this year, we need to build that sense of camaraderie so we can gel as one."

I nod. This is something different that we haven't done before, but I like the sound of it.

"Adams," Coach Andrews calls out to me, "since you're excited, you'll be down on that end of the ice."

I follow his finger and wait as he divides up the team. Marcus and one of the new guys, Ryan, join me, while Noah, Dax, and one of the rookies take the other side. The assistant coach tosses a ball my direction and blows the whistle.

"Remember, you can't hold on to it for more than three seconds."

Tossing the ball to Ryan, I skate forward and watch as he throws it to Marcus. He heaves it in my direction before I duck under Noah. Before I can pass the ball, the whistle blows.

"Too long, Adams. Fields's team gets the ball." He skates in a line as he watches us play. "Imagine this is a puck. Work with your teammates. See where your competition is on the ice. Constant awareness."

Nabbing the ball from Dax out of thin air, I'm faster this time in sailing it over Noah's head to Marcus. With only the rookie in his way, he chucks it straight into the back of the net.

We're jostling each other, having fun, but Noah's team takes a quick lead and we can never quite catch up. They end up getting beat by the last team, meaning all of us still have to do line drills.

"We tried." Marcus skates up to me. "At least we'll all suffer together."

"Doesn't make it any easier, Cap."

Coach claps his hands. "I like what I'm seeing, men. I'll see you all tomorrow. We'll start in the weight room before working on our lines."

"Can we play more handball?" Jasper asks.

"Damn. Jasper having fun?" Graham chides him. "Never thought I'd see the day."

He flips him off.

"We'll do more of this, yes. Now hit the showers."

I skate off the ice, not wanting to be out here any longer.

The first day of practice is always hard. No matter how much training I put in during the offseason, it pales in comparison to the work our coaches put us through. The fact that I didn't puke like a few of the rookies did makes me feel better.

Add to that practice a baby who decides when I sleep, and I'm gassed. I'm one of the last ones in the locker room. Heading straight to my stall, I sit down, stretching my legs to let my muscles have a break.

"How do you feel?" Marcus asks.

I peek one eye open at him, leaning back against my locker.

"I feel like a Zamboni ran over me."

Marcus claps me on the shoulder. "You'll get used to that feeling. I eventually did."

"Really?" I shift, pulling my jersey up and over my head.

He nods. "It felt like the girls didn't sleep for the first year I had them. If one was asleep, the other was awake. I felt like a zombie."

"You know,"—Jasper comes up to the two of us— "you're not making a case for having kids."

"It's hard to mind when you love them," Marcus says on a sigh.

"It really is. I'm a sucker for that little face," I say. "Even when he's crying, he somehow manages to look adorable."

Jasper shudders before stalking back over to his locker. "No, thanks."

Marcus elbows me in the side. "Listen, if you want to bring Caleb over and have dinner with us, we can give you a break. The kids would love to dote on him."

I smile at him. "I might take you up on that."

"Please do. Harper is starting to get baby fever, and maybe if Caleb is fussy, I can hold her off for a little while longer."

"You don't want more kids?" Dax asks from Marcus's other side.

"We do, but I'd like to enjoy some time with my wife."

Harper got pregnant right after they renewed their vows, so I can understand them wanting to wait. I lived my life never wanting to settle down. It didn't feel like something I was ever going to do.

Now? Now it feels like I've settled down in a different way. I never knew that a tiny bundle of chaos could change my life the way he has.

Staring at the picture of the two of us I printed out and hung up, I smile.

Yeah, I'm okay with the different kind of chaos life has thrown at me.

Chapter Eight

BODE

I'm exhausted. I have never been more exhausted in my entire life. Even my eyelashes are tired.

Caleb was up all night for the second night in a row. I never knew a baby that size could poop so much. I had to get more diapers and wipes delivered this morning because I went through everything I had.

At least the vomiting stopped.

I called the pediatrician, but they weren't concerned. The nurse told me what signs to look for and to make sure he stays hydrated, so that's something I am keeping a close eye on.

Which is something I never thought I'd be doing.

Right now, the baby in question is staring up at me, tears wetting his eyes.

"What's wrong, buddy?"

His lip quivers before a rip cuts through the air.

"Oh, fuck." I gag. The smell is terrible. Probably the worst thing I've smelled in my life. Well, since last night at least.

Sighing, I get up and carry him upstairs to change him. I've lost count of how many times we've done this.

I know I can change a diaper with the best of them now.

"Is this bothering you too?"

His tiny bottom is starting to get red, so I slather more diaper cream on it to try and help. Poor kid is miserable.

That makes two of us.

And there goes the doorbell. Who in the world is here in the middle of the afternoon on a Friday?

Gran and Deb left after watching him this morning while I had my workout, and Stevie is currently at the spa. She asked if she could stay and help, but I promptly sent her to work.

I have no idea if this is a bug or not, but I don't want Caleb getting everyone sick. The one good thing so far is he doesn't have a fever.

"Let's go see who's at the door."

I toss his dirty onesie into the laundry basket and grab a fresh one to put on him when we get downstairs.

For now, he's clean and not crying. That's all I can ask for.

Pulling open the front door, my jaw drops. "Miss Mitchell. What are you doing here?"

A dead panic washes through me. What is going on? Is there a reason she just randomly decided to show up? Did I do something wrong?

"It's Friday. I had a follow-up visit scheduled with you."

"Friday?" I rack my brain, trying to figure out what day of the week it is, but it's all blending together. "But today…"

"Is Friday," she finishes for me.

"Shit," I mutter.

When I got home from practice—on what, Wednesday?—Gran said Caleb was spitting up more than normal. I kept a close eye on him, but it only got worse. Between him getting sick and diarrhea, I'm past knowing what my name is, let alone the day of the week.

I forgot about this entirely.

"Come in." I hold the door open for her, sweeping my arm out to welcome her in. "I'm sorry, but the house is a mess. Caleb is sick today."

Following her into the living room, I look around the main floor of the house. God, if I were her, I'd question my ability as a father.

A pile of laundry that needs to be folded is sitting on the counter. Probably the first of many loads today. Empty bottles sit next to the fridge. The package of diapers that I opened earlier looks like it has exploded across the living room floor.

Caleb has been so miserably unhappy that I haven't put him down since I got home, so I haven't had the chance to clean up.

Hell, Caleb isn't even dressed as I'm holding him in my arms.

"How are things going?"

"Honestly?" I let out an exasperated sigh. "Terrible. The house is a mess. I wish I had four sets of hands and about eighteen more hours in a day to get everything done because I feel like I've been doing nothing but changing dirty diapers. And I worry every single day if I'm the right person to raise him."

Shit. That was way more than I ever should have dumped on this woman.

"Sorry." I wince.

The woman smiles at me. "If you told me everything was great, I'd be more concerned."

"And you're not now? Should *I* be concerned?"

She gestures to the living room and we each take a seat. I take the onesie from my hand and get Caleb dressed.

"It's been close to two months since Caleb arrived. No parent learns everything overnight. But all I see here is that you're trying. If you really didn't want to be his father, you would have insisted on a paternity test the day I showed up rather than waiting to do one to clear up paperwork for the state."

I didn't need the results of said paternity test to know that Caleb is mine.

Caleb is sitting in my lap. His expression is clear, but for how long, I don't know. That dimple of his—the one that matches mine—pops out when a smile graces his face.

Fuck, I love it. Even sick, he is the cutest thing I've ever seen.

"I've been waiting for the day when I regret taking him in. When I realize it's too much to be raising a kid, but it hasn't come. I love him."

Miss Mitchell smiles at me. "I'm glad. Being a parent is the hardest job in the world. My two children are grown, and I still worry about them."

I chortle. "Great. So this feeling is never going to go away then?"

She shakes her head. "I'm afraid not. You can only hope you raise them well so they are a good person."

I press a kiss to Caleb's head. It smells like the baby shampoo I use. A smell that calms me. "I hope he's a better person than I am."

"From where I'm sitting, you're a good person."

"Thank you."

Coming from an almost complete stranger, that means a lot. Because this woman does have a lot of say over what happens with Caleb. The fact that I'm his biological dad goes a long way. But if things weren't going well, she could take him from me.

It instills a fierce protectiveness in me.

I will do whatever it takes to make sure my son has the best life possible.

With me as his father.

Chapter Nine

BODE

I think he's asleep. I start to move and he doesn't stir.

Thank God.

Shifting Caleb in my arms, I walk as slowly and quietly as possible toward his crib and lay him on his back. He lets out a soft breath, his little face heavy with sleep.

I can't help but stare down at him. It's been a couple of months, but it feels like I've finally got a hold on these things.

Now, when he cries and I pick him up, he cuddles into me. Maybe it means he likes me? God, I hope it does because I'm realizing I'm starting to like this dad gig.

Fucking love.

Heading out of his room, I shut the door and jog down the stairs. The house is quiet. Looking out at the pool house, it's dark. Knowing Gran and Deb, they're out.

Who knew she would have more of a social life now than I do?

Grabbing a few beers from the fridge, I head out into the warm night. The heat of the day has finally loosened its stronghold and it feels comfortable.

Stretching out onto one of the pool chairs, I crack open a bottle and take a long pull.

Fuck. This feels good. My body is tired from practice. Getting back into workouts after the offseason is always hard. Especially now that I'm doing it on so little sleep.

The chirping of cicadas fills the air. Fireflies are lighting up the early night sky. Taking a deep breath, I revel in the peace. It feels good. No, great even.

This isn't something I ever thought I'd want. Before Caleb, I never would have thought about spending a night at home by myself. If I was, it usually was because I couldn't find anyone to hit up the bars with me. I always liked having someone with me. Made it easier to pick up women. Didn't hurt that I was a hockey player.

It makes me sound like a dick, but they knew the stakes. They knew what they were getting with me—one night, no strings attached. That's how I lived my life.

No emotions. No attachments.

I now have the biggest attachment of all.

Checking the baby monitor, I smile at the sleeping kid. He really is cute.

The back door opens and closes followed by the sound of flip-flops slapping on the flagstone. I turn to see Stevie illuminated by the lights spilling out of the living room, making her look like an angel.

"Hey."

I don't want to startle her, but she jumps anyway.

"Oh, sorry. I didn't see you there." She turns back toward the house. "I don't want to bother you."

"Hey, join me." I grab one of the beers and hold it out to her.

"Really?"

"I wouldn't mind the company."

She grabs the bottle and plops down into the seat next to me. "Thanks."

"Cheers."

"I feel like I should be buying you beers," Stevie says, taking a sip of her pale ale.

"Because I'm letting you stay here?" I ask, quirking a brow at her.

She laughs. A warm sound that feels like bourbon on a cold night. Soothing and sweet.

"I meant because I was going to use your pool. I can't remember the last time I went for a swim."

"Oh, right. Well, you're welcome to use it."

The thought of her using it? Stripping down to a bikini? It has dirty things rolling through my head. Things I definitely shouldn't be thinking about.

"Listen, I don't know much about you. Tell me something." Stevie's eyes sparkle in the quickly darkening night.

"What do you want to know about me?"

She laughs. Again with that laugh that does funny things to my insides. "You were terrible at getting-to-know-you games in school, weren't you?"

I shrug a shoulder. "I was great at my favorite hockey player, but it didn't come up much."

"Okay, so who's your favorite hockey player?" She quirks a brow, bringing the bottle to her lips and taking a sip.

Does she realize what she's doing? The mind games she's playing with me with one innocent move?

Stevie may look pure enough, but I bet there's a devious streak inside her.

"Bobby Orr."

"I don't know who that is."

I groan. "Of course you don't. God, I have so much to teach you."

"Sorry. If you want a favorite Spice Girl, or which version of *Pride and Prejudice* is better, I'm your girl."

"*Pride and Prejudice?*" I ask. Now I'm the confused one.

"You don't know *Pride and Prejudice?* You never read it in school?"

I shake my head, gulping down my beer. "If we had to read something in school, it was likely that I got the summary online."

"You missed out."

I nod. "How about an easy one. Favorite game?"

Stevie sets down her beer and folds her legs together on the chair. The T-shirt she's wearing slides down her arm, exposing the graceful line of her shoulder. All that tender skin there is begging to be sucked.

Shifting on my chair, I push that thought out of my head.

"I'm *very* good at games. Sorry is my best game. I always win."

"You always win? I don't believe you."

"I'm serious. Sorry is my jam. If I had it with me, I'd kick your ass tonight."

"Well, maybe if we played The Game of Life, I'd kick your ass."

"That is all luck," Stevie points out.

"How is Sorry not?" I throw back at her.

"It's more strategic. Which piece to move once you get out."

"Keyword *once* you get out," I tell her. "Luck."

"So you think."

I smile at the woman sitting next to me. Who knew it could be so fun talking about board games?

"Favorite sports team?" I ask.

The grin splits her face. Her hair is piled on top of her

head, and sitting here in the soft, evening light, she looks stunning.

"Black Diamonds."

"A knife through the heart." I feign hurt. "I can't believe you said that."

"It's the only team I could think of. My friend Crestina's fiancé is from Denver and loves them."

"Well, you'll have to bring them over and we'll convince him otherwise."

"Deal." She smiles back at me. "Here's one for you. Favorite meal to cook?"

"Oh God." I bury my hands in my face. "This is embarrassing."

"Let me guess…you're not a chef?"

"No. I have a nutritionist prepare all my meals for me. I figure it's easier than trying to cook for myself."

"Hmm." Stevie's beer bottle hangs from her fingertips. A pensive look washes over her face. "Filing that away for later."

"What do you mean later?" I ask.

"Well, I have a go-to meal that I'm great at cooking. I don't get a chance to make it very often, so maybe I can teach you something."

"Nice. I mean, fun. Good." I cough, trying to cover up the bumbling idiot I've become. How can one woman turn me into such a mess? "That sounds good."

Stevie is clearly trying to hold in her laughter. "Great. It's the least I can do. I can't let poor Caleb starve when he gets older because his dad can't cook."

"Hey. He's not even nine months old yet. Let's not go turning him into a teen just yet."

Stevie drains the last of her beer and reaches for another. "Mind if I have one more?"

"Sure."

"I know you didn't get Caleb all that long ago, but is it weird thinking of him growing up?"

I peel at the label of the bottle. "Yeah. I mean, he's this tiny little thing, but his personality is already starting to come out. Is he going to be like me? More like his mom?"

"What were you like in high school?"

That has laughter bursting out of me. "God, I was terrible. I think I gave Gran more gray hairs my junior year than she's gotten her entire life."

"I can see it."

"Hey. I can't imagine little Stevie was a saint back then."

"I was." She waggles her eyebrows at me. "I couldn't stand the thought of getting yelled at, so I never got into trouble. Never broke curfew. Never drank. I was an angel."

"Of course you were. I'm picturing you in the library during school, doing your studying and getting ahead on homework."

"There was nothing wrong with trying," she defends. "I was never a great student, so I had to work. I hated school."

"Is that why you're an aesthetician now?"

"More or less. I enjoy what I do."

"Tell me about it." Shifting in my chair, I turn to meet her gaze.

"I like people. I like getting to work with them and help them if they're having trouble with their skin. I want to help them feel beautiful."

"I'm sure you are good at that. And what makes you feel beautiful?" The words are spilling from my lips before I can stop them. I can see the question catching her off guard.

"Right. I should probably get to bed. I have an early

day tomorrow." Stevie grabs her empty beer bottles and hops out of the chair like it lit her on fire.

"You don't have to go." I jump up, trying to stop her but she's faster. She's scurrying inside before I can convince her to stay.

Damn it.

The night air is choking now, so thick I can see it. Just when I thought we were having a real conversation, she runs off.

I want to know all about this woman. Every scrap. Every seed. Anything she'll give me.

How can I be so taken with one woman I barely know?

Sighing, I gather up the remaining beer bottles and head inside. After spending this little time with Stevie, I realize I have to take my time with her. Something has scared her off, and I want to know what that is.

I will figure out my roommate if it's the last thing I do.

Chapter Ten

Coward.

That word is on repeat in my head as I walk inside the building that houses the spa.

The minute things started to get too comfortable with Bode last night, I fled.

We were having fun, talking about things that didn't matter. But the second it turned personal? I tucked my tail between my legs and ran. Because I didn't want to delve into anything too personal about me.

Bode is too much. Too sexy, too much man, too much everything for me to spill my secrets to. One shred of who I am and he would go running in the opposite direction.

That's the last thing I want.

Right now, staying with him is keeping me together. It's giving me a semblance of a life. Like I'm a real adult. I don't want to do anything to rock the boat.

"Hey, girl."

I jump a foot in the air as Cressy enters the locker room. "Jesus. You scared the crap out of me."

She looks at me like I've lost my head. "I said your name like three times."

"Ugh. Sorry." I bang my head on the hardwood of the locker. Lavender and bergamot perfume the small room. The soft sounds of the meditation music fill the air. "Lost in my thoughts."

"About a certain player?"

"What? No."

She eyes me with a wide gaze. "If you weren't so jumpy, I might believe you."

"You try living with someone so gorgeous."

Cressy sets her bag down and pulls her short, brown hair into a ponytail. "Oh honey, I have my own sexy beast at home."

"Yeah, but you're in love with him. Mine is just tormenting me."

"Aha!" She points a perfectly manicured finger in my face. "So you admit he's sexy."

I roll my eyes. "Of course he is. Have you seen him?"

"Well, that's step one in admitting you have a crush."

"Who says I have a crush?" I question.

"Please." Cressy waves me off. "It's easy to see."

"I told him when I first moved in that he has nice skin. I mean, who does that?" I slap my palm against my forehead.

Cressy shrugs as we slide into our smock tops with the spa logo on them. "I mean, you work on faces every day. It's a natural thing to notice."

"And to blurt it out to him? Hmm?"

She laughs, bumping her hip into mine. "Well, I guess not completely normal."

Tying my hair back, I slide into my work shoes and take off toward the lobby. "I have other things to worry about besides the man I'm living with."

Like not getting so wrapped up in another person that I lose myself. I hate that I keep letting this happen. Why do I get so taken by a pretty face and forget who I am?

No. That is not going to happen again.

No matter how much I might be attracted to Bode.

My lady parts need to stop reacting and keep their feelings to themselves.

"Mrs. Jones. How are you?" One of my longtime clients is waiting for me in the quiet waiting area. "How was your visit with the grandkids?"

She gives me a big toothy smile as she follows me to my private suite.

"Can you believe that Ben is five now? It seems like just yesterday he was a tiny baby. I got my workouts in chasing after him every day. It's exhausting."

I laugh as I close the door behind her. "It'll be nice that you can have some time just for you."

"I need it. I'm getting some new dry spots I need you to work your magic on."

"You know the drill. I'll step out while you get settled on the table with the sheet over you and I'll be back to work my magic." I wink at her and move into the hall.

Several people are moving through the halls, clad in robes as they go into the various rooms for their appointments.

The soft music hums overhead in the dimly lit space. The ambience, right down to the soothing smells, makes for a relaxing day. It's even relaxing for us, the employees. I don't know who could have any troubles working here.

"You ready?" I knock on the door, waiting for a response.

"Yes, dear."

I step inside my room, which is filled with everything I

could possibly need for the various kinds of facials. Lotions. Oils. Extraction tools.

"Alright. Let's get your skin glowing again."

Dimming the lights, I get to work.

BY THE TIME I'm stepping inside the house after seven, I'm exhausted. I love what I do, but it doesn't mean working on people all day is easy. You have to be careful about all sorts of reactions to products and different skin types, so you need to be on your game.

Kicking off my shoes, I follow the sound of voices into the kitchen.

Papers are spread out all over the island. Nan and Eve are sitting at the bar with glasses of wine. Caleb is sitting in Eve's lap as Bode is hunched over something with a red marker. Pizza boxes sit under the cabinets along the wall.

"Stevie, dear. How was work?" Nan spots me and greets me with a smile.

"Good. Sorry, didn't mean to disturb."

Bode's eyes travel up my body, making me feel things as his gaze locks on to mine.

Stop it, Stevie. Stop feeling things for the sexy man you're living with.

"Grab some pizza. We're just going over my travel schedule for the season and planning who will be watching little man."

Caleb coos as Bode tickles his stomach.

"You sure?" I set my bag on the counter.

"There's plenty."

"Thanks." My stomach gives a rumble as I find a plate and grab a few slices. Biting the tip off, I give a happy sigh.

Veggie pizza. My favorite.

"Okay. We have bridge on the fifteenth that month. We can't miss it."

I hold back my laugh. Of course their schedule revolves around bridge.

"Shit. Okay. Well, that will be the last away game on that road trip, so maybe I can see if Harper can watch Caleb that night. I mean, what's one more kid when you already have three?" Bode laughs.

I set my plate on the granite surface and eye the calendars laid out. "I'm actually free that day if you want me to stay with Caleb."

Bode shakes his head. "You do not have to help."

"Hey. I don't mind helping out. It's the least I can do."

"Are you sure? He can be moody when he wants to be."

I grin at the baby who looks anything but moody. A smile is etched on his face. He's looking at his dad like he's his favorite person in the world.

"Yes, he really does look like a handful, Bode," I tell him, a note of sarcasm in my voice.

"Wait until he starts screaming at three in the morning for his bottle."

"Has he ever done that? Because I never hear a peep from him."

Bode smiles at me. "Guess that means I have good insulation. He wakes me up every night."

I shrug a shoulder. "Not the end of the world a few nights a week."

"Not even a few nights. A couple of days tops."

"I can do it."

"Stevie. Isn't that so sweet of you?" Eve says. "Tell her how nice that is, Bode."

Bode rolls his eyes at his grandma, and I can't help but laugh. "How nice of you."

"I ought to smack you upside the head," Eve tells him, shaking her head.

"Gran. You say it like I wasn't going to thank her anyway. I wasn't raised in a barn."

"Some days I don't know."

"You know you raised me, right? That's a dig on you."

She waves him off. "Are you sure you want to help, Stevie? You have to deal with this guy."

I look to Bode again, but it's brief. The last thing I need is for these two old women to catch any hint that I might be attracted to Bode.

With the kind smile and warm eyes. The sexy hair that always seems to fall over his forehead. The scruff that lines his jaw that I want to feel in other places.

I clear my throat. "I can handle it."

At least, I hope I can handle it. Because being surrounded by Bode is something even a saint would have trouble dealing with.

Chapter Eleven

"You want to go for a drink tonight?" I ask Crestina, getting ready to head out. "I need to unwind after today."

She shakes her head, slinging her bag over her shoulder. "I can't tonight. I have dinner with Dylan's parents, but maybe tomorrow?"

"Sure." I hang up my smock and shut my wooden locker. "I'll see you later."

"Love you, babe."

"Love you too," I call out behind me. Pushing open the back door of the employee entrance, a wall of humidity slams into me. It's a steamy night in Nashville. Music floats in the air as the first tendrils of darkness start to thread the sky.

The last thing I want to do right now is head back to Bode's. Not only did I want to hang out with Crestina, but the thought of being around him is too overwhelming.

The light scent of his soap.

His hair swooping into his eyes.

Everything about him is effortlessly sexy.

Not wanting to go out by myself, I resign myself to going home.

Bode's home.

Shoving the key into the lock, I open the car door and plop down into the seat. My entire body heaves a sigh of relief to be done with work. I love what I do, but some days are harder than others.

Today was one of those days.

Ornery clients. Some wanting upgraded services without paying. Others didn't leave tips.

Rolling down my windows, I blast a new tune from the singer Genevieve and point my car toward the suburbs. At least I don't have to fight mad drivers as I leave the city behind me.

I sing along to the catchy tune as I get closer and closer to Bode's place. Genevieve exploded onto the scene, and I'm addicted to her music. I can't carry a tune to save my life, but I sing at the top of my lungs anyway.

I turn the volume down as I punch the code into the gate in Bode's neighborhood and wait for the heavy iron gates to open.

Parking in my spot, I grab my purse and head inside. The outside lights glimmer as a few lamps are still lit inside. Knowing what time it is, I'm guessing Caleb is already asleep.

The sight that greets me as I walk inside is too much. Bode is stretched out on the couch—shirtless—with a sleeping baby on his chest and wearing a pair of gray sweats.

This. This is the reason why I didn't want to come home. Heat is simmering in my veins at the sexy man in front of me. I was hoping one drink at a bar might have meant that Bode would be asleep when I got back, because

I know that the minute Caleb falls asleep, Bode isn't far behind.

"Hey," I whisper.

Bode looks back over the couch at me and holds a single finger over his mouth.

"Hi," he mouths. Standing, Bode waves at me to sit on the couch. "Give me a minute."

I nod and watch as he goes upstairs. I try to keep my eyes on his back, but that's hard when his ass looks incredible in those sweats.

Bode Adams is the most perfect specimen of man I've ever seen. But I live with him and I absolutely don't want to act on that.

Maybe if I keep telling myself that, I'll eventually believe it.

"Sorry." Bode jogs down the stairs and collapses on the couch next to me. "He's starting to cut more teeth and is miserable."

"Poor thing. Are you doing okay?"

"I leave in two days for my first road trip, and the thought of leaving him guts me."

"He'll be in good hands. I know all three of us are going to be here."

"I wish I didn't have to leave him," Bode confesses. "It makes me feel like a terrible father. Like I'm letting him down in some way."

"I've been around you long enough to know you aren't letting him down at all. Caleb loves you."

"Can I tell you something?" Bode whispers.

His bare feet are stretched out on the coffee table, hands clasped over his bare stomach and the slab of muscles there.

"Sure." I nod.

"I never had a mom growing up. At least, not that I can remember. Gran was the only role model I have."

"Really?"

Bode nods, turning his head to look at me. His brown eyes are heavy as his head rests along the back of the couch.

"My mom left when I was a baby and my dad when I was ten."

"Wow."

"The two of them leaving made me the man I am today. I never heard I love you from my dad. Haven't seen him since he dropped me off with my gran one day and never came home."

"I—"

"I don't need your pity," he cuts me off.

"I wasn't going to say that. I was going to say you and I are more alike than you know."

"Really?"

I tuck my feet under my butt and sit facing him. I'm close to him, my knees brushing against his thigh.

"Neither one of my parents wanted me either."

"How could anyone not want you?" Bode asks. His large, warm hand drops onto my knee, and it causes all the feelings swirling around inside of me to become a jumbled mess.

Lust.

Anger.

Sadness.

Desire.

It's too much, but it has me confessing even more to him.

"My mom was always working two jobs because my dad split when I was five. She blamed me for it. Said I ruined her life. Made her feel worthless. Ugly. Finally, when I was a teenager, I moved in with Nan. I couldn't take it anymore and petitioned the state to become an emancipated minor."

"Really?" Bode asks.

"Really. When I told my grandma that's what I wanted to do, she stepped in and took me in. I haven't seen my mom since."

And it explains why I bounce from relationship to relationship. Always settling for any man that gives me a scrap of attention. It's also why I want to make my own way and not stay here for free.

Sure, Bode might not need my rent money, but I don't want to leech off his generosity.

"I guess you and I really are alike," Bode tells me. "I'm sorry you went through that."

"I wouldn't wish it on anyone. Doesn't make growing up easy."

"Really?" Bode squeezes my knee. "It kind of turned me into a dick."

"Yeah?"

He scrubs his free hand over his face, hiding the wince. "I slept my feelings away with anyone I could. I'm not proud to admit it, but it was easier than facing the fact that no one loved me."

"But you have Eve," I point out. "Surely she told you she loved you."

"She did. But it's different, you know? I was already abandoned at that point and it didn't really help."

I drop my elbow onto my knee and rest my head on my fist. "I was the same way. I mean, not falling into bed with any guy, but anyone who looked at me and said I looked pretty, I fell for. Hook, line, and sinker. Guys wanted the quiet, pretty one. The second things started to get serious, they dumped me."

Bode's finger traces a circle on my knee. I don't even think he knows he's doing it. "They're idiots."

"You're just saying that."

"No." Bode's hand cups my cheek. "I'm serious, Stevie. You're so much more than just the pretty one. And I'm not just saying that."

I've never bared my soul like this to anyone. Bode is the only person I've felt safe with. How can I confess my darkest secrets to the man I only met a few weeks ago? The secrets that make me feel less than. That hammered into my psyche just how unlovable I really am.

"I always tried to be the badass, but no one ever saw me like that."

Sinking his fingers into the hair at the nape of my neck, Bode pulls me close. His lips press against my forehead, and I relish the warmth that spreads through me.

Something I've never felt before.

"You're so much more than anyone has ever made you feel. More than just your looks. I haven't known you for that long, Stevie, but you're incredible."

Emotions clog my throat. How can one man's words slip into the cracks and help heal them? I shouldn't need another person to tell me this, but sometimes, it's hard.

It's hard to make yourself believe something when all the evidence points to the contrary.

"Thank you." I press a kiss to his temple. "Thank you, Bode."

"If you need the reminder, you know where to find me. Last bedroom on the right." He winks at me, and it helps the heaviness in my chest ease.

"I should get to bed." I thumb toward the stairs behind me. "I have another early day tomorrow."

"Right. How about I make us dinner tomorrow as a

thank you for helping out? Our grans will be out at bridge, so we'll have the house to ourselves."

"Only if you let me help. Considering you said yourself how abysmal your cooking skills are."

Bode holds out his hand and I take it. "Deal."

His hand is warm and rough under my soft one. I want to feel it everywhere.

Bode has captivated me in the worst possible way.

And I'm finding I don't mind in the least.

Chapter Twelve

STEVIE

"What are you doing in here?" Nan asks, walking into the kitchen with Eve hot on her heels.

"Bode and I are making dinner tonight. Figured I'd get ready while I feed Caleb."

Eve lifts him out of his chair and swings him around. "While your Gran is going to go win big tonight."

"Only if Betty isn't there," Nan points out.

Eve rolls her eyes. "Cheater that she is. If she knows what's good for her, she won't show her face."

"Now, now. Save that energy to beat everyone in bridge."

I pop a carrot in my mouth before setting Caleb's dinner on his tray—well out of his reach after watching Bode's disaster.

"I have to earn my grandbaby's college tuition." Eve smacks a kiss on his cheek then straps him into his high chair. "Love you, baby."

"Don't get into too much trouble," I call out after them.

Knowing them, they will get into a lot of it. But that's for them to figure out and not me.

I hear another voice in the mix and butterflies take flight in my stomach.

Bode.

It's hard to feed Caleb his peas when he becomes more interested in his dad coming home. I try to wipe the mush off his cheeks, busying myself to calm my nerves.

God. I wish this man didn't make me feel like this. Having that heart-to-heart with him? Kissing him? Well, his temple? Not good judgment.

"There's my favorite little guy." Caleb's happy shouts fill the kitchen when Bode walks in. I track the sexy man with his eyes as he plants a kiss on top of Caleb's head. "What are you eating for dinner? Is that peas?"

"And carrots." I chomp down on my own. "Although I think these might be better."

Bode smiles at me and damn it. Is he doing that on purpose? He has to know what that smile does to me. It's unfair how good it is.

"I see you took your promise about showing me how to cook seriously."

"Well, I figured we could whip something up that will be good for you before your game tomorrow."

"And what's that?" Bode asks, rolling up his sleeves, taking Caleb's dinner bowl and feeding him the rest.

"Sausage and spinach pasta. Easy enough that you should be able to get the hang of it."

"Sounds good. How are we going to make it?"

"I'll get it started, but you worry about Caleb."

Bode nods. "Okay. Easy enough."

I dump tomato sauce in my pan and let it start to simmer as I grab another pot to start the water boiling.

"What are you making?" Bode asks.

"I like homemade sauce. A little garlic, some carrots for more veggies. Onions."

"Sounds like no kissing then."

My cheeks flare with heat at his words. I lean my face over the pan on the stovetop so I can blame the flush on the heat.

Bode saying those words is too much. I can't take it. Because I want to be kissing him.

Get it together, Stevie.

Shaking those thoughts from my head, I start to brush all the vegetables from the cutting board into the pan so they can cook.

"It smells good," Bode says, coming to stand next to me.

"Thanks. It's a go-to of mine. Easy to make and filling."

"How'd you get into cooking?" Bode asks.

When the sauce starts bubbling, I add the sausage and cover the pan with the lid.

"It came easy to me. I felt like it was the one thing that I was good at, so why not keep doing it?"

"You know," Bode starts, "you're more than just good at cooking."

"Oh yeah?"

"I mean, I still have to see that you're good at board games."

I laugh, stirring the pasta into the boiling water, then covering the pot and leaning back against the counter. "You sound skeptical."

"Because no one is *good* at board games."

"So you think."

"So I know," Bode clarifies.

I wave the straining spoon at him. "See if I help you cook anymore."

That earns me an eye roll. "Fine. You're good at board games."

"Hey. I'm going to kick your ass when I find my box of games."

Bode sits down on the barstool next to Caleb and cleans the remnants of peas and carrots from his face.

"I look forward to it."

His brown eyes are playful. The quirk of his lips makes him look sexy as hell. Why is it everything this man does lights me up?

I wish I could suppress these feelings.

I sigh as the water starts to bubble over. At least cooking dinner will distract me.

Getting the rest of the food ready while Bode takes care of Caleb is easy.

"Here."

I pass a hearty bowl over to Bode and give myself a heaping portion. It smells too good not to indulge. Fishing the cold bottle of wine out of the fridge, I pour myself a glass and take the seat next to Bode.

"This smells delicious."

I stab my fork into the noodles and take a very un-lady-like bite. "Mmm. I was so ready for this."

"Damn, this is good," Bode says, taking another big bite.

"I'm glad you like it," I tell him. "Are you ready for the season?"

"I think so."

"How's the team looking?"

Bode drops his fork into the bowl and props one leg up on the stool between us. Caleb is in his arms, playing with the toy he now has.

"Did you look up things to ask a hockey player?" A smirk plays on his mouth.

I shrug, turning my attention back to dinner. "I mean, maybe."

"That's really fucking cute."

"What? I had to have something to ask you."

"Please tell me you know it's a puck," Bode begs.

"Of course I do. I have seen a hockey game before. I've never been to one, but I would watch the occasional one with Nan."

"Wait." Bode leans forward, shifting Caleb onto his other leg. His little hands find Bode's bowl and Bode pushes it out of reach without thinking. "Does that mean you knew who I was before you came here?"

"What? No. Nan would watch it at the retirement center because it was on. I think this was before she met Eve?"

"Sure."

"If I had something to throw at you, I would."

Bode laughs. "Well, maybe we could find some more of Caleb's dinner if you really wanted."

"Tempting."

"Please don't throw your dinner at me."

I shake my head, looking at the man next to me. "I won't. I like it too much to waste it on you."

"Ouch. A knife through the heart. Guess I won't wave to you guys on TV tomorrow."

"Well, we'll all be watching. Whether you wave to us or not." I laugh.

"I always get nervous before the start of a new season. I know it's only preseason, and we're heading to New York, but will everything we've done carry over to the game? Are we going to play like shit? I want to win it all, and it's hard to push all of that to the side when the puck drops."

"Do you tell your teammates this?"

He shakes his head. "No. I don't want them to think I don't trust them or us as a team."

"Well." I squeeze his arm before taking my hand back. The less contact, the better. "You can talk to me about it. I'm here for you."

"So I can tell you I'll miss Caleb like crazy tomorrow." He presses a kiss to the top of his head.

"I would be worried if you didn't."

"I'm glad I can leave him with people I trust. If I didn't have you or Gran, I don't know what I'd do."

"Like I said, we're all here for you."

"Thanks, Stevie. I'm glad you're here."

"Me too."

I mean it. Even if it's going to damn well kill me being in the same room as this man, I'll do it. Because I like Bode.

And that's a truth that's hard to admit after everything I've been through.

But a truth, nonetheless.

Chapter Thirteen

BODE

The mood is electric. Even though it's only a preseason game, everyone is pumped.

The start of a new season.

It's early. The game doesn't start for another hour, but the place is packed. People are crowding around the glass, hoping to get a signed puck from one of their favorite players.

"You ready, man?" Jasper is next to me, shooting pucks toward our goal as we warm up on the ice.

"Fuck, yeah."

Championship banners line the walls in the arena. More than half a dozen retired jerseys sit next to them.

New York is one of the great hockey teams. Even when they're having a bad season, their fans are always supporting them.

Us? Nashville has their die-hard fans, but these new fans that keep coming on board? I don't want to lose them.

It's a good feeling having the support of the fans behind us.

I want us to have a banner ceremony one day. I want it so badly, I can taste it.

"Looks like some fans made the trip." Marcus skates over to us, his stick resting on his shoulders. A group of kids in red jerseys are waiting by the tunnel where we'll head back to the locker room before the game starts.

I wave at them and watch excited grins spread across their faces.

"Holy shit. Look at you interacting with kids." Jasper's jaw is practically on the ice. "I don't think I've ever seen you do that."

"Fuck you." I nail him with the butt of my hockey stick. "I'm nice to people."

"There's a difference," Marcus clarifies. "You're nice to them, but I don't think I've seen you wave at kids before."

I shrug a shoulder. "Well, things are different now that I have Caleb. I wouldn't want people being a dick to him."

"Okay, seriously. This whole nice guy thing is weird." Jasper cringes. "I seriously don't know if I can handle it."

I smile at him—the fakest smile I've ever given him. "If the kids weren't watching, I'd flip you off."

Jasper smiles back at me. "There's the Bode we all know and love."

"Hey, I contain multitudes now."

"Listen to you and the big words," Jasper jokes. "I think you're finally growing up."

"Only took him his whole life." Marcus skates off as the whistle blows and we're beckoned back toward the locker room.

Fishing a few of the pucks off the ice, I toss them over the glass toward the kids.

"Thanks, Bode!"

Three happy faces stare back at me, waving. I wave as I

head toward the visitors' locker room. Once I'm there, I'm too hyped to care how stark the room is. That's the way it is for visitors—but we don't need it to be fancy.

We're here to play a game.

"Alright, gentlemen. First game of the preseason." Coach Andrews steps into the locker room in a finely pressed gray suit. The overhead lights are glaring off his bald head. His coke-bottle glasses make his brown eyes look bigger as he scans the room.

"We've been working hard and looking good in practice, but it means nothing if we can't put together a solid game."

"So much for a pep talk," Noah mutters under his breath next to me.

"I like what I'm seeing. We've got a good team. One of the best I've worked with, and I'm not just saying that to blow smoke up your ass. I want you to go out there and leave it all on the ice. Not just tonight, but every game. I don't want you to have regrets that you could have played harder when you look back."

I nod, feeling the familiar buzz move through me. The energy of the arena is rocking, even from here. This is why I love hockey—the way we can put everything out of our heads and focus on the game.

Right now, in this moment, nothing else matters. Everything going on in my personal life is pushed to the side.

I can't worry if Caleb is doing okay or when his next teeth are going to start coming in. I can't think about my gorgeously sexy roommate.

The only thing that matters is the puck and starting this season on a high.

"New York is a good team. They have the crowd on their side. I want you to work as a team and go out there and show them what we're made of. Even though we were one win away from the finals last year, we're still the underdog tonight. Let's go out there and prove them wrong!"

"Hell yeah!" someone shouts as Coach pulls us all toward the center of the locker room.

"Knights on three. One, two, three…"

"Knights!" we echo, grabbing our sticks and helmets and heading back toward the ice for the puck drop.

We're announced to boos from the home crowd, as expected. There are a few clusters of red, proudly repping the Knights jerseys, but they are far outnumbered in the sea of dark green.

When the lights go down, the crowd erupts. A warrior's song, like Vikings going into battle, announces the home team lineup. I recognize most of their team. A few new faces that got traded, but I've come to know a lot of these guys playing against them over the years.

Even had a few nights out with some. We leave everything on the ice. After? We can hang out and have a beer together.

After the anthems are sung, Marcus calls the starting lineup together.

"Alright, boys. We've been through a lot together. I want us to make this the best season, okay? You heard what Coach Andrews said. Leave it all on the ice. I love you guys."

"Let's do this!" Noah fires back before we break the huddle and take our starting positions.

The puck drops and Marcus tries to grab it, but New York is faster. It's easy to see their skill, but Noah is already setting up, stopping them from making it into our zone and shooting the puck back toward Marcus.

He sends it over to me and I fly down the ice. Dax is

neck and neck with me as I pass it to him, but before he can get it and send it back to Marcus, New York stops us.

"Damn it."

I push after them, but they slide by our defensemen and get the puck in the back of the net.

It's an easy goal to start the period.

One that we get back after Graham stops them and sends the puck to Jasper. The bar down goal is a thing of beauty, clanking off the cross bar and sailing down into the net.

"Nice job, old man." I clap him on the helmet as he slides onto the bench next to me.

"Careful who you're calling old. I'm only two years older than you."

"Ancient in hockey." I wink at him before hopping over the boards for a shift change.

New York is able to put the biscuit in the basket before the end of the first period, and we come out ready for action. Dax scores on a deflected pass and I get the assist on a beautiful pass to Marcus before the end of the second period.

It's a slog toward the end of the game. We're evenly matched and fighting for every inch gained on the ice. We're still hanging on with a close lead, 3-2, as the minutes tick away.

That's when my chance comes.

An errant stick deflects the puck. Grabbing it from our zone, I take off down the ice. There's only one defenseman to beat as I deke him out.

Now it's just me and the goalie. Watching as he settles into the goal, I fake right then left and fire it into the net.

The lamp lights up and a collective groan issues from the home crowd.

"Hell yeah!" I pump my fist as the guys all pile on to congratulate me.

"Nice work!" Marcus bumps my shoulder pads with his fist. "That was a thing of beauty."

Damn. That felt good.

Skating to the bench, I slide in the open gate and take my seat.

"Nice work, Adams." Coach taps my helmet. "Way to read the play."

I nod, swigging my water and watching as the remaining time fades away, earning Nashville our first win of the season.

The mood in the locker room is raucous. Everyone is ecstatic that we managed to beat the home team day one.

"Great job, men. Take tonight to enjoy this win and then tomorrow, we'll start preparing for our game against Boston."

I answer a few questions for the press waiting in the locker room before I get cleaned up and back into my gameday suit, ready to make the short trip to Boston.

The buses are waiting for us as I jog up the stairs and take my usual seat.

"How was the first game away from Caleb?" Marcus asks, sitting down next to me.

"Honestly? I miss him. Is that weird?"

He's been out of my life longer than he's been in it, but he's already wormed his way deep inside my heart.

I also miss Stevie, but there's no need for me to tell him that.

"Not at all. I'd say you get used to it, but you don't. I miss the family something fierce when I'm gone. Even worse when we can't video chat beforehand."

I smile at him. "At least you can. I don't know if Caleb would understand what is going on."

"He'd probably want to eat the phone."

"Sounds about right."

The bus pulls out and I settle in for the trip.

I feel good. A win to start the season?

Yeah, this is a high I want to hold on to for as long as possible and keep it going through the season.

And maybe it's the sign of good things to come.

Chapter Fourteen

BODE

> Get some rest. Caleb and I will be watching tomorrow night

That has me wanting to puff out my chest and bring home the win just for them. Stretching out onto the queen-size bed, I ignore the too-firm mattress beneath me.

Would I rather be at home hanging out with Caleb and Stevie? Absolutely.

But I love my job, so that means I'm here with the guys tonight in another hotel room that blends into all the rest.

"Open up." Banging on the door echoes in the hotel room.

Fuck. I just lay down, my entire body giving a happy sigh. The first game of a road trip is always hard, and New York is a tough team. All I want to do right now is lie down and go to sleep.

I have a feeling the one thing I'm going to like about these road trips is sleeping through the night. No crying baby to wake me.

Dax opens the door and the guys pile into the room.

"We're playing video games tonight," Graham tells us, unceremoniously.

"Really? Aren't you exhausted?" I ask, moving over on the bed when Jasper whacks me in the thigh.

"Can't keep up anymore, old man?"

"Who you calling old, Jasper?" I jab.

He flips me the bird as he sits down next to me.

"We need a little team bonding," Noah tells us.

I roll my eyes. "You know, you can say you just want to hang out. You don't have to do it under the guise of team bonding every time."

"Would you say yes otherwise?" Noah quirks a brow at me.

Fuck, he does have a point. I know it's the only way to get Marcus on board, based on the face he's making. I know he would rather stay in his room and call Harper and the family, but clearly he lost that battle.

"I don't know how you have the energy. I mean, Dax here took that wicked hit in the second," I tell them.

"That means we do what I want to do," Dax says, giving us all a smile that lights up his baby face. Poor kid doesn't look older than a teenager, thanks to the facial hair he can't grow. Something I've heard him whine about too often since we room together.

"So video games it is," I say, resigned.

Any other night and I wouldn't mind. All I wanted to do tonight is crash. I had a quick call with Gran while we were on the bus and heard all about Caleb's night.

It's weird how much I enjoyed hearing about the mundane things he did. Like eating peas.

Who would've thought I would have been so engrossed in a kid eating peas? Seeing as how he's thrown them at me every time I've tried feeding them to him, I'm ecstatic.

Noah and Graham fire up the game as Dax takes a seat next to them.

"How's Caleb doing?" Marcus asks from his seat near the window.

"He's good. Great, actually." I pull up my phone and find the picture Gran sent me tonight. He's sitting in his floor seat with a tiny Knights onesie on. "Look how cute he is."

Marcus looks at the picture and then looks back at me. "You're just like any other parent now. Showing pictures of your kid to anyone that asks."

"I can't help it when he's the cutest fucking thing ever."

"Harper has to stop me from oversharing pictures of Jamie." Marcus laughs. "Literally, the kid could puke all over me and he'd still be adorable."

I rear back in disgust. "Okay, having gotten spit up on the other day, I can confirm that is not cute at all."

"Can you two stop talking about kids puking?" Dax yells out, twisting his body as his character does another lap in the game. "No one needs to hear about this."

"Hey." Marcus chucks a piece of popcorn from the bag he's eating at the back of Dax's head. "This is what you talk about when you have kids."

"If you two start talking about poop, I'm leaving," Jasper tells us.

"I mean, if it gets you guys out of here faster..." I trail off.

He cuts me a mean glare. "Don't even think about it."

"Hey, if I win the tournament, everyone is out."

This is how it always goes when we play video games together. We take turns competing against one another until there's a winner. Usually, everyone has to buy them drinks that night, but we never actually follow through.

Mainly because Noah and Graham duck out early, and Marcus never comes out because he wants to call his family.

Which, now that I have my own son at home, I can't blame him. I'd rather stay in than go out and celebrate a win.

"See if you can do better." Dax pops up, mumbling about an unfair loss and hands me the remote.

"Oh, I will." I give him a cocky smile.

Because now that I'm in control of the game, I plan on winning so I can go to bed. Like I wanted to before these guys came to interrupt my plans for the evening.

Marcus grabs the controller from Graham and the two

of us take our starting positions. It's a game I've played too many times to count. I could play it in my sleep. We learned early on that we can never play hockey games because we got into a fight and Dax nearly got his nose punched in.

Hockey players aren't competitive at all.

I take an easy lead, Marcus not putting much effort into his lap at all. Knowing him, he knows if he gets out of here sooner, he can go call Harper.

"You have to at least try, you dickhead." Noah punches Marcus in the arm.

"I am!" he defends. "It's not my fault I'm terrible at this."

I roll my eyes at him. "You're not terrible. You just don't want to be playing."

Marcus leans back onto the bed, dropping onto his elbows. "You're right, I don't. Can't we just say Bode wins and all go to bed?"

"Seriously, you are a grump," Graham tells him.

"Not a grump," Marcus corrects. "I have a very hot wife waiting up for me, and I'd rather see her than your ugly mugs."

"Ouch." Dax feigns hurt. "It's like you don't love us."

"More like I love my wife more."

"Get out of here." Jasper smacks him on the back of the head. "I'll take over for you."

"Don't have to tell me twice." Marcus flies off the bed like a bat out of hell. We can't get a word in before the door is closing behind him.

"Damn. Apparently he misses her," Noah points out.

"It's not like everyone travels with their partner," Graham tells him.

Noah gives Graham a chaste kiss. "Aren't we lucky?"

"Is everyone in love?" Dax whines.

"Technically it's only those two." Jasper doesn't look at us as he easily takes the lead from me.

Shit. I really need to be paying better attention. If I win, I'm definitely kicking these guys out. But because I want to go to sleep, of course it takes another hour for me to finally claim victory. It's easy to enjoy the night with these guys because they're like family, but right now they're a very annoying family that doesn't want to take the hint and leave.

"Alright. I'm kicking you guys out," I tell all of them.

"Ugh, fine," Noah groans. "I'll take Graham on when we get back to our room."

"How do you still want to play?" I hold the door open for them, not letting anyone linger.

"We'd invite Dax with us, but he's looking exhausted too," Noah says as he pulls the door shut behind him. Dax is already asleep, hand resting on his stomach.

I shake my head at them as they all file out. The minute the door closes, it's silent. Just what I want. Exhaustion has well and truly taken over as I collapse face-first into the pillows.

"WHAT THE FUCK WAS THAT?"

Looking around, the room is cloaked in darkness. Dax lets out a grunt from the bed next to mine.

"Dude." Reaching across the small space in the room, I smack his arm. "Did you hear that?"

"Hear what?" he groans.

"That noise."

"I have no clue what you're talking about. Why are you awake?"

Glancing at the alarm clock, I see it's just after three in the morning. "I don't know. Something woke me up."

"And you felt the need to wake me up?" Dax rolls back over, facing away from me, and pulls a pillow over his face. "You're just mean."

Nerves are roiling through me. I don't know what it is or what I heard—or *thought* I heard—that is making me jumpy.

Grabbing my phone, I unlock it and navigate to the app that Harper had me load. The one that connects to the video monitor in Caleb's room.

It's hard to make him out through the slats in his crib. Is he even in there?

Shit. Maybe that's what made me panic.

Is Caleb okay?

I don't think before hitting Gran's number on my favorites and waiting for her to pick up.

"What in the hell are you doing calling me this early in the morning?" she says by way of answer.

"Is Caleb okay?"

"What?" Her voice is muffled. "Why are you calling? He's fine."

"I can't see him."

"Because he's sleeping."

"Gran. Can you please go check on him for me?"

I hear her huff out a breath. "You know he is just fine."

"Oh my God. Would you go into the bathroom? Some of us are trying to sleep here!" Dax yells, throwing a pillow my way.

"I don't know who that is, but I agree with them."

"You two are being ridiculous," I tell them, tossing the comforter off me and stalking toward the bathroom.

"We're being ridiculous?" Dax calls out after me.

"You're the one waking everyone up because you had a bad dream."

"It wasn't a bad dream," I mutter to myself.

"Then why are you calling?" Gran asks.

I close the bathroom door behind me and put her on speaker so I can pull up the monitoring app again.

"I can't check on my kid?"

"Not when it's two in the morning."

"Please?" This time, my voice is softer. Maybe if she hears me pleading, it'll make her want to help.

"Only because you asked so nicely."

If I could see her, I know she'd be rolling her eyes at me.

"I love you, Gran."

"Yeah, yeah." Light spills out from her opening the door. "You know, in my day, we didn't have these fancy contraptions to let you see your baby when they were sleeping."

"Did they have electricity then?" I ask her.

"I should whoop your ass for that comment and hang up right now."

"Hey, you volunteered to do this," I point out.

"Did I? I don't recall that."

"Pretty sure you said you'd help when you moved in."

"It's too early to remember what I agreed to," she whispers. I can see her in Caleb's room, a casual flip of her middle finger sent to the camera.

"Real mature, Gran."

"If you wanted mature, you would've called Stevie."

"Is he okay?" I ask. "The sooner you answer me, the sooner you can hang up."

"He's fine."

"Fine as in still breathing?"

She huffs. "Yes. He is fine. I'm going back to bed."

Ending the call, she cuts me an evil glare through the monitor and leaves his room.

Fuck. Is this what being a parent is like? Constant dread and worry? Maybe it'll get easier with each road trip.

But what if something happens while I'm gone?

Would Stevie think I'm ridiculous if I call her tomorrow night? Probably not. She'd go check on him, let me know how he's doing, and that'd be the end of it.

No middle fingers or argument.

Now I wish I was able to call and talk to her. She's only been with us a couple of months, but it's like she's been in my life so much longer. I never realized how nice it would be to have someone like her around.

She's gorgeous. A knockout, really. But it pales in comparison to how big her heart is. She's seen me at my worst and didn't turn away.

Her soft smiles and warm glances are what keep me going on the hard days. She makes me feel like I can do this whole parenting thing.

Fuck.

Now I really shouldn't be thinking about her like this. Because the memory of running into her in the hallway, in just a towel no less, is living rent free in my head even after all this time.

And not just my head…

I really need to get it together, because I don't want to scare her off. She's one of the few people that knows me for me and likes me.

I want to keep it that way.

Chapter Fifteen

STEVIE

"Hi, hi, hi!" Cressy bursts in through the unlocked front door. "Did I miss kickoff?"

I snort a laugh as I hold out Caleb's spoon for him. A lovely mix of sweet potatoes and peas. "You mean the puck drop? No."

Caleb giggles, slapping his hands on his high chair tray.

"See?" Cressy sets the bottle of wine down on the counter. "Caleb thinks I'm hilarious."

"He's nine months old. I'm pretty sure he'd be entertained if a ghost came into the room."

"But he couldn't see a ghost."

"I can't with you sometimes." I nod toward the plastic wineglasses sitting on the island. "Pour us some and I'll get Caleb washed up."

Cressy comes and stands next to me. "He really is a cute kid."

"He is. He's such a happy baby." Using his spoon to wipe the rest of the food off his face, I clean him up before pulling him out of his high chair. "Yes, you are."

I coo and gush over him as I grab the hummus and

chips from the fridge, balancing it in one hand with Caleb on my hip. The pregame show has ended, with the lights now flashing across the ice.

"Where are they playing tonight?" Cressy asks. I hand her the plate and she sets it on the coffee table before settling back in the oversized cushions with her white wine in hand.

"Boston, I think? Could be wrong, but Bode's been gone for a week now and his schedule has all blended together."

"A week? He can leave this cutie for that long?" She tickles Caleb's side, earning her a laugh.

"It's not like he can stay home."

"So his live-in…roommate," Cressy questions, "is also his nanny?"

"What? No. I'm helping him out."

Dunking a cracker into the hummus, she shovels it into her mouth. The starting lineup is announced and Bode's sexy face flashes across the screen.

"Okay, how are you living with this man and not jumping his bones?" Cressy asks. "If I weren't in love, I'd hate you."

"Stop it." I bounce Caleb on me as he chews on the icy toy to help his incoming teeth. It seems like he's getting more and more nowadays.

"I'm serious. That man is hot."

"And you think I need to be dating the man that I'm living with? Please. That is the worst idea ever."

"No." Cressy sips her wine. "The worst idea ever would be not making good use of your time here and crawling into bed with him."

"You can't say that around Caleb!" I cover his ears. Not that he would understand a word of what we're saying, but the sentiment still stands.

"Fine. You should have s-e-x with B-o-d-e while you l-i-v-e here."

"Now you're just being mean." I poke her with my toe.

She winks at me. "Only trying to get my point across."

The puck drops and Marcus shoots it over to Bode. Bode takes off down the ice, working with the other guys on his line to set up the play. I don't know much, nor do I know all the intricacies of the game, but it's fast. So fast, I almost miss when Bode puts the puck in the net.

"Yes!" I shout, grabbing Caleb's arms and waving them in the air. "Daddy scored."

He's celebrating on the ice as his teammates crowd around him. The hometown team is booing him, a few even flipping him off from behind the glass.

"He made that look easy," Cressy tells me.

"He's good, right?"

"You can say that again."

Boston ties the game before the end of the first period, and easily scores at the beginning of the second. The Knights don't take it lying down.

Between Jasper, Marcus, and Bode, they move the puck down the ice. Jasper to Bode to Marcus back to Bode across to Jasper before he sends it flying to Bode and it's in the back of the net.

"Wow. Two in one night? That's pretty good," Cressy says as the score gets tied up again.

"It is." A grin stretches across my face. I love watching Bode play. He's so good, and his love for the game is evident as he skates back to his line for the puck drop.

Caleb falls asleep in my arms as the game continues. Boston scores again, but Marcus quickly scores another Nashville goal to tie it up again.

As the third period starts, shots are fired, but defended with ease by the goalies.

"Okay, why do people like sports? This is way too intense for me." Cressy is leaning forward, chewing on her perfectly manicured nails.

"This isn't even that bad."

There's still ten minutes left in the game. It takes less than a second to score— another thing I've learned.

Noah grabs the puck that's blocked by their goalie and fires it toward Bode. He's off, skating down the ice on a breakaway. There's no one in front of him as he dekes out the goalie and puts it in the back of the net.

"Yes," I whisper, not wanting to wake up the baby in my arms.

"Holy shit. That was incredible," Cressy tells me, turning to look at me. "You two look so cute."

She pulls her phone out and snaps a pic, then holds it out for me to see. I smile at the photo as I listen to the commentators.

"Bode Adams with the goal. He is on fire tonight with a hat trick. He's really stepping up as the playmaker this season. If the Knights are looking for someone on the ice, Adams is always there," the commentator says.

A surge of pride courses through me. Since the season started, I've watched almost all of Bode's games. It's hard not to get hooked on the game. The way Bode skates is mesmerizing. It's like he's one with the ice. It's hard to take my eyes off him.

Not that I even really want to.

Bode Adams is too damn sexy for his own good and he's a temptation that is getting harder and harder to deny.

"Well, it seems that the commentators love Bode," Cressy points out.

"He's an amazing player," I tell her.

"That's the only thing we're recognizing right now. Okay."

"If I didn't love you, I would kick you out right about now."

"Ouch." Cressy feigns hurt. "I see where I stand."

"Yeah, yeah."

"Okay, okay. Back to the soccer game."

"Hockey." I laugh.

"Fine, hockey. I have to tell you, they keep showing their coach, and let me tell you, you could also date him. He's hot for an older guy."

"You're hopeless; you know that, right?" I sip my wine before grabbing my own cracker and way too much hummus.

"Hey, I'm determined to find you someone that is worthy of you. My bestie deserves the world."

I drop a peck on her cheek. "And that's why I love you."

Kicking my feet out, I settle in to watch the game, Caleb snuggled up in my arms. It's a lot of back-and-forth, something I've learned about hockey since I started watching.

As time winds down, Boston does what they can to try and close the lead, but to no avail. Nashville walks away with the win, 4-3.

"Wow. That was fun." Cressy glances down at her phone. "It's getting late. I should probably go."

"Hang on. Let me put Caleb down and I'll walk you out."

Seeing as how he's already asleep, he doesn't fuss as I put him in his pack 'n play while I clean up the dishes and walk her out. I'm sure he'll wake up when I change him, but I'm hoping he'll go down easy.

"Thanks for letting me come over tonight."

I hug her to me. "I had fun."

"See you at work tomorrow." Cressy pecks my cheek before she heads out to her car.

Shutting the door behind her, a smile spreads across my face. Tonight was good. Easy. It seems like it's been a long time since I've been able to just relax and not worry about what's going to happen. I mean, Cressy kept poking about Bode, but that's never going to happen.

Lifting Caleb into my arms, I take him upstairs to put him to bed. He wakes and starts to cry, so I quickly change him and drop into the rocker to hopefully get him back to sleep.

He's a spitting image of Bode. Caleb is going to grow up to be a heartbreaker just like his dad.

My phone buzzes in the pocket of my sweatshirt. Pulling it out, I smile at the name that lights up the screen. Dimming the display, I unlock it and go to my texts.

BODE

Did you watch the game?

I know it was late

STEVIE

We did

<<photo of me and Caleb together watching game>>

Fucking adorable

Both of you

Couldn't even keep him awake with a hat trick

Maybe he'll stay awake next time

Cressy and I had fun though

Your friend?

Yes

Was it okay she came over?

Totally fine

Can't be any worse than having our
grandmas there 😅

Oh, they're off at bridge night

I was told not to wait up for them

Of course

Hopefully we don't have to bail them out of
jail 🚓

That's on you if we have to do it

Maybe a night in the slammer will do them
some good

I'm confused now

Are we hoping they get arrested now?

Maybe

But not if I lose my childcare

I'll make sure Caleb is taken care of

Then let's hope for it

Fingers crossed

Speaking of fingers crossed...

I was actually hoping you might want to go
out when I get home

> Like…a date?

Yes, like a date, Stevie

I want to take you out on a date

HOLY SHIT. Bode wants to take *me* out on a date? Oh God. I try not to let the panic overwhelm me. I can't scream or freak out because Caleb has fallen back asleep in my arms.

I don't remember the last real date I went on. When I met my last boyfriend, we went on a handful of dates and then I moved in. It devolved into a few meals here and there at home and occasional orgasms. For him, never me.

The thought of going out with Bode? What if he gets to know the real me and doesn't like me? Whatever good feelings I had from earlier tonight are being pushed to the side by nerves.

STEVIE

> Omg!

CRESTINA

What?

> Bode asked me on a date!!

> Me!

And you're telling me this why?

Other than the fact I love you and am not jealous at all but am madly in love with my own fiancé

> Stevie: I can't say yes, right?

If you say no, I am unfriending you
right now

Gee, thanks

Why are you even questioning this?

Because of my last relationship

It wasn't even a relationship

He was a dickhead who clearly didn't see
how amazing you are

I SIGH, sinking back into the oversize couch. All the lights
are off, except for the TV flashing across the large room.

BODE
Soooo....

STEVIE
Yes

You sure?

Yes

Can I ask you anything right now and you'll
say yes?

Stevie: No

Damn. And here I thought I could work this
to my advantage

You got me to say yes to the important
question

What else is there?

So much more, Stevie

So much more...

OH GOD. His words send heat licking up my spine. Saying yes to the date was easy. Saying yes to more? I don't know if I'll be able to.

I'm far too into this man. I want him so badly, and I don't know if I'll ever be able to recover if Bode walks away.

Maybe I'll just have to learn to say no...

Chapter Sixteen

STEVIE

"Are you sure this looks okay?" I hold the phone in the mirror so Crestina can see the outfit I'm wearing. It's nothing fancy, simple really.

It's a plain black cardigan that dips low, tucked into wide-leg jeans, finished off with a brown, woven belt and black ankle booties. I stack the few gold chain necklaces I have to make it look a bit nicer.

"Babe, you look hot. Like *hot* hot. Bode is going to lose his mind when he sees you."

"It's weird, getting ready to go out when I live down the hallway from him."

"So?" Cressy shrugs a shoulder. "Maybe it'll make the tension hotter when he sees you."

"This isn't a nineties rom-com. It's not like I'm going to shake out my hair and suddenly be different."

Cressy scoffs at me. "I meant more like he's seen you with no makeup on and he'll think you look hot."

"Okay. I'm going to let you go. I need to finish getting ready."

She points a finger in my face. "I better not hear from you tonight. Only tomorrow. With details. *Lots* of details."

"Goodbye." I stab the end call button and toss my phone onto the bed. Of course she would say that.

I take my time applying my makeup, having a thorough routine since I work on faces all day. Not only that, I want to look good for Bode.

It seems like so long since I've been on a date. I've been at Bode's almost two months now, and it's hard to fathom not being here. I've gotten comfortable staying with him. Not to mention, it's nice seeing Nan more.

Setting my makeup in place, I take one last look in the mirror.

Deep breaths, Stevie.

You can do this. It's only dinner.

Spritzing on my perfume—the fanciest thing I own, being a designer brand—I grab my phone and head downstairs.

Soft voices waft up the stairs. Turning onto the landing, I see Bode on the floor with Caleb as our grandmas sit on the couch, chatting.

Even from here, I can tell Bode looks good. The way his dark jeans hug his legs. Hockey does wonders for that ass.

"Stevie. Look at you."

Eve's voice pulls my attention to them as Bode spins around and pops up.

"Wow. You look…great." Bode clears his throat as he meets me at the bottom of the stairs.

"So do you."

Bode looks edible in that white button-down of his. The top three buttons are undone, exposing his chest. With his shirt tucked into his dark jeans, and brown oxford shoes, he looks super sexy.

So fucking delicious, I want to take a bite of him now.

Down, Stevie.

"Don't you two make a cute couple," Nan gushes, walking over to us with Caleb in her arms.

"Nan!" I hiss.

"What?" She shrugs her shoulders. "No harm in pointing out the truth."

"Now, make sure you don't come home too early," Eve says. "Maybe cause a bit of trouble while you're out."

Bode groans next to me. "Gran. You know I can't get into trouble. That would look bad for the team."

"I have no intention of getting into trouble," I tell her.

She waves us off. "You two are no fun."

"Yeah, try and have some fun on your date. If you even know what that is," Nan snickers.

"You want to get out of here?" Bode asks, ignoring them.

"God, yes."

Bode drops a kiss on Caleb's head as we head toward the garage. Grabbing my purse, we're in Bode's truck before they can follow us, likely to make fun of us again.

"Has your Nan always been like that?" Bode asks.

"Yes. What about yours?"

"For as long as I can remember."

"It's a wonder we turned out so normal then." I laugh. "Where are we going tonight?"

Bode waits for the gate to open before easing into traffic. "There's this little French place I found that has great reviews."

"Okay."

Conversation with Bode is easy as we head toward downtown. The skyline is already lit, even with the sun still out.

Pulling up to a building not quite in the thick of Broadway, Bode valets his truck and comes to my side to help me out.

"Oh. This looks nice."

Bode smiles at me and holds open the door of a three-story brownstone building. Lamps sit in each window, hidden behind linen curtains.

Bode gives his name and we're ushered to a row of tables along one wall. A heavy chandelier hangs from the center of the room. The floorboards creak beneath our feet. The light from the candles on the tables and the chandelier cast everyone in shadows.

"Thanks." I smile at Bode as he pulls out the chair for me before taking his seat.

He opens the menu, giving it a casual perusal. Bode looks at ease here. Looking around, all the couples are dressed to the nines. Women are wearing pearls and the men are in suit jackets.

I feel wholly underdressed. It's places like this that always make me feel like I don't belong.

"Welcome to Le Jardin d'Étoiles," our server greets us. "We're happy to have you join us this evening. Can I start you off with something to drink?"

My eyes almost bug out of my head when I glance at the wine list. A glass of wine almost costs what I make in a day.

"Can we have a few minutes to look the menu over?" Bode asks.

He bows to him in his white tuxedo shirt and black suspenders. "Take your time."

"Anything stand out to you?"

"Umm…"

"What?" That has him worried.

"The menu is in French. Do you know what any of this means?"

"Hang on." Bode grabs his phone and taps a few buttons. "Here, see if this translates it."

"Thanks." I smile at him from across the table. The small flicker of candlelight makes him look even sexier. If that were possible.

"Is it helping?"

"I don't really know what anything is."

Ingredients are so elaborate, I have no idea what they are. I mean, what is mousse cracker?

"I thought I saw steak online," Bode confesses. "That's usually what I get."

"There's steak tartare, it looks like. But I don't know if that's the same thing."

That earns me a laugh from Bode and a glare from the couple sitting next to us.

"I don't think so."

"It's not that I don't appreciate you bringing me here, Bode, I do, but—"

"But this isn't your kind of place?" he interrupts.

I nod. "Sorry."

"Shit," he mumbles, setting his menu down. "Can I tell you a secret?" Bode whispers, leaning over the candle sitting between the two of us. We're so close to the other tables here, it feels like I'm bumping elbows with them.

"Yes."

"I've never really been on a date."

"You haven't?"

That surprises me. The man oozes sex. I don't know how he would have any trouble finding someone to take out.

"I mean, in high school, we went to the football games and did group hangouts. As an adult? I won't go into the details."

I wince, knowing the details with that one sentence.

"Well, if it makes you feel better, I don't need to be wined and dined at a fancy restaurant."

"Yeah?" Bode closes his menu. "Want to get out of here?"

"Yes."

Bode links his hand with mine, jogging down the stairs as we run out the door. "Okay, if you don't like fancy French places, can you give me a hint of what you do like?"

Stuffing my hands in the back pockets of my jeans, I spin on my heel to face him.

"Something fun."

"Fun?" His face lights up. "Okay, fun I can do. Let's go."

Chapter Seventeen

BODE

"This is more my speed." Stevie smiles up at me, wearing a big, cheesy grin as she adjusts her vest.

"Good thing I know for next time."

Stevie steps closer to me, the tips of her boots touching my tennis shoes. I changed into the pair in my truck when I got to our new spot for the evening.

"You have to beat me in order to win a second date."

I tip my head closer to her. "Is that right?"

"Gotta work for it."

"Do either of you two need pointers on how laser tag works?" The young girl working the front desk draws our attention back to her.

"Point and shoot?" I joke.

She chomps her gum and nods. "Yes. Through those doors. The lights will turn green when it's time to start."

"Roger that." I salute her and grab Stevie's hand to head into the room I booked for the two of us at a small laser tag place near the restaurant.

I should have known that restaurant wouldn't be Stevie's kind of place. I put so much thought into taking her somewhere special that I didn't even think if she would like it.

Fucking idiot, I chide myself.

But seeing her happy face now? I'm okay with this change in plans. It's more me if I'm being honest with myself.

"You think you can beat me, Bode?" Stevie asks.

"Oh, I know I can."

If it means getting a second date with her, I'll do everything in my power to win.

"You're going down, Adams," Stevie calls out.

The minute the light turns green, I'm ducking behind an oversized black mountain of sorts that's lit up with pink lights. Other games are going on around us, but I'm trying to keep my eyes peeled for a certain blonde.

A few teens run by and at the end of the line is Stevie. Before I can jump up, she's diving under a log and aiming her gun in my direction.

"Nice try!" Stevie calls out.

I pop out and move deeper into the room. I'm in the open too long and Stevie gets me, one of my lives flickering out.

"Ha." Her voice echoes around the room as strobe lights flash and the bass from the music thumps around the room.

I'm laughing as I find protection in a tiny-ass cave. I barely fit, but do my best to curl up and wait her out.

There is no way I'm losing in laser tag.

Especially with a second date on the line. Even if my legs start to fall asleep.

"Come out, come out and play, Bode." I hear her voice.

Peering out from my hiding place, I see there's the smallest opening and I shoot, hearing the noise of success.

"Damn it!"

"Now, now, Stevie. Language."

"Funny, coming from you, Bode," she tosses back at me.

This is what I should have planned from the start. Having fun and goading each other.

I'm not a fancy guy. I don't need a hundred-dollar steak and wine. This is better than I could have imagined.

Stevie makes another run for it and I get her easily.

"You only have two lives left, Stevie. Do you really want to lose to me?"

"I don't plan on it, no."

"So confident." I get stuck trying to leave my hiding spot, and Stevie gets an easy two shots on me, resulting in her having one life over me. "Clearly you didn't think this one through."

I army crawl to another safe space and wait as neon lights start to flash. With her having more lives than I do, I need to be strategic.

A flash of blonde hair runs by with kids in front of her. Making my move, I see her vest light up as I duck behind a tree-like structure for protection.

One more to go.

There's a recharge station where groups are hanging around—the only safe space in the whole game area. Neon tape marks it off on the floor, and seeing that Stevie is now on the outside of it, I fire my last shot at her.

Raising my arms, I'm victorious.

"Hell, yeah!"

"That wasn't fair." Stevie walks over to me, poking me in my vest-clad chest. "I was recharging my gun. That wasn't allowed."

"You weren't at the station. You were by it."

"Technicality," she huffs, walking out of the dark room.

The overhead lights in the lobby have me shielding my eyes it's so bright.

"Still won, baby." I wink at her.

"You cheated!" she scoffs. "That's not fair."

"I did no such thing." I blow the tip of my laser gun as I revel in my win.

"You totally did. I want a rematch."

"Stevie, Stevie, Stevie. I never thought you'd be such a sore loser."

Placing her hands on her hips, she stares up at me, trying to be fierce. But something in her blue eyes is preventing it.

"I'm not a sore loser if you cheated."

Before she can walk away, I grab her hand and pull her close. "How about next week then? I did win…"

She eyes me up and down. "Because—"

I slap a hand over her mouth and watch her eyes go wide. "And don't say it's because I cheated. I won fair and square, and that means I get another date."

Stevie mumbles against my lips, but I don't hear a word of it.

"Sorry, what was that?"

"Another date? Yes. But I think we might need to take laser tag off the table."

My heart swells in my chest as I wrap an arm around her shoulders and lead her toward the equipment return.

"I will put it on the no-go list along with fancy French restaurants."

"I won't say no to some dinner. I believe I was promised some."

I shake my finger at her. "I believe I said a date. I didn't specify dinner."

Stevie sidles up to me and wraps her arms around my waist. There's a slight flush to her face from running around. Although, it has me imagining that from more pleasurable things. "If I admit defeat, will you feed me?"

"Yes." I stow the electronic gun and vest and open my locker to grab my wallet and keys. Looking around, I see the teenage girl at the concession stand, handing out slices of pizza. "How does that sound?"

Stevie still has a grumpy look on her face as she nods.

"What do you want?" the girl asks.

"Three slices of pepperoni for me, and…"

"Two sausage for me," Stevie answers. "And two cherry sodas, please."

"I ran out of plates. Want boxes?"

"Sure thing." I tap my card on the reader and drop a twenty-dollar bill into the tip jar.

She places the greasy slices into two to-go boxes, puts them in a bag, and fills up Styrofoam cups to the brim with dark liquid and thanks me.

"Want to eat outside?" I ask, taking the plastic bag of food.

"Sure." Stevie grabs tiny packets of Parmesan cheese and napkins before grabbing the cups and following me into the parking lot.

Clicking the lock on my fob, I open the passenger door for her and help her in.

"Oh look, you can be a gentleman." A smirk plays on her beautiful face.

I lean close. So close I can see her eyes darkening. "Oh, you want a gentleman? I can show you just how gentlemanly I can be."

Before I make my next move, I shut her door, round the hood, and hop into my seat.

She has the drinks set in the cupholders with napkins sitting on the console between us. Pulling two boxes out of the plastic bag, I toss it into the back seat and set our culinary masterpiece between us.

"Not quite a French masterpiece, but I think this will do."

I cheers my pizza to Stevie's as I take a big bite. Fuck. There is nothing better than greasy pizza.

"An Italian feast." Stevie winks at me as she tears off the tip of hers.

I sprinkle the cheese over the top of my slice before taking a slurp of my drink. "How'd you know I like cherry soda?"

Stevie turns, tucking her knees up on the leather of the seat. "I took a guess. It's my favorite."

"Good to know we have something in common."

I won't get into the shared trauma of our childhoods. We don't need to bring that up on a first date. Maybe it's why we connected so easily.

"Okay." Stevie licks the grease from her fingers and sets her slice down. "Since you've never been on a real date before, how would you rank this one? How do you think you did?"

"Taking into account the failed French restaurant?" I grab a napkin and wipe my hands off.

She nods. "Yes. Even that. And the cheating."

"You were outside the neon tape! It was a good hit."

She wads up her napkin and tosses it at me. "It wasn't in the spirit of the game."

"That's not how we count goals in hockey."

Stevie gives me a fake smile, leaning over the console. "I know how I'm ranking this date. Zero out of zero stars."

"Well, then that's basically a glowing review."

"Crap," she mutters. "I meant five stars."

"Nope." I shake my head. "No take backs. One hundred percent for the star pupil."

"You're incorrigible."

"If it helps, I give this date five out of zero stars."

Even in the dim light in the cabin of my truck, I can see Stevie smile. A real, happy smile. Something I'm starting to learn I really, *really* like.

"Five hundred perfect? I don't think I've ever scored so high."

I shrug a shoulder. "I mean, if we're going on technicalities of math, anything times zero is still zero."

Resting her elbow on the dash between us, Stevie beckons me closer. "I like five hundred instead."

"Anything else you like?"

I shift closer. The air intensifies around us. I can feel the energy between Stevie and me. I want to pull her closer to me by the V of her cardigan and take her lips in a searing kiss, but I don't.

Not until she makes the first move.

Her eyes dart down to my mouth and back up. I don't know if she realizes what she's doing, but she's taking in my entire face. As if she's memorizing every detail.

"Stevie?"

I can't take it anymore. I need to taste her lips. To see if it's as good as I've been imagining.

"Yeah?" It comes out as a breathless whisper.

"Can I kiss you?"

"Yes, please."

I smile at her before sinking my hand into her soft hair. Finding the rubber band, I pull it out and finger the soft strands. It's like silk as I press a soft kiss to the corner of her mouth.

Moving to the other side, I kiss that corner. Rubbing a thumb over her bottom lip, I study her face. Her breath hitches, eyes widening with desire.

I savor everything about this moment, stroking her cheek, before closing the distance. My lips seal to hers.

With one touch, I'm a goner. Absolutely and totally fucked because it's the sweetest, yet best kiss of my life.

Swallowing her gasp, I slide my tongue into her mouth and savor the sweet taste. Every mewl and whimper has me sinking my hands into her hair and tugging her closer. I'm ready to throw caution to the wind and hoist her into my lap and fuck her here and now.

But she deserves more.

Even if it's good. So damn good, I'm losing my mind.

Needing a breath, I pull back, but Stevie doesn't let me go. Leaning over the console, she knocks the pizza box to the ground and captures my lips in the hottest kiss of my life.

Holy. Fuck.

I want more. More of this. More of Stevie. I've never felt anything like it before. I'm not sure why this woman is bringing out these emotions, but she is.

Each brush of her tongue against mine has my cock thickening in my pants.

Clasping her cheeks in my hands, I slow her down.

"So." Kiss. "Fucking." Kiss. "Good."

I capture her lips in a warm kiss. Sweet. Teasing. Taunting.

I could stay here all night and not get bored, perfectly content just like this.

But reality buzzes in my pocket.

"Shit." Grabbing my phone from my pocket, I go to silence it, but it's Gran.

GRAN

Caleb is starting to fuss and we're out of
Motrin. Any chance you could pick some up
on the way home?

BODE

Sure thing

I think it's his teeth again

Okay. We'll be home soon

"SORRY. Caleb isn't feeling too well."

"Is it his teeth?" Stevie asks.

I love that she knows this and I don't have to think of some excuse to ditch her. Not that I would want to, but she understands my life.

"She thinks so. Want to finish off the date by stopping by the drug store and going home to snuggle a teething baby?"

Stevie pecks one last kiss on my lips.

"Yes." Leaning back, she picks up the pizza and finds the bag to dump it into. "And just so you know, this date just went up to six hundred percent."

"Then next time I'll try for seven hundred."

Chapter Eighteen

BODE

Finally.

After what feels like hours, Caleb is finally asleep. These last few weeks have been miserable. With his teeth coming in, he's been in pain and it is a knife through the heart hearing his whimpering cries.

I don't know if I could have made it through without our grandmas and Stevie's help. Between my schedule and practice, I've been spending every minute at home when I'm not at the rink. And if I'm gone, it's one of them stepping up.

We've got a stretch of home games this next week and I'm thankful. The last thing I want to do is leave a fussy baby with others.

Now that the cooler nights are upon us, I swipe a sweatshirt from my room and jog down the stairs.

Stevie is in the kitchen, pulling a container out of a brown paper bag.

"Hey."

She startles. "Oh, hi. Looks like Caleb is down."

Pointing at the monitor I left on the counter, she pries

open the lid of a plastic container. The smell of enchiladas wafts over to me and I take a deep breath.

"Got any of that you can share?" I ask.

She glances at the clock. "Don't you normally eat when you get home from practice?"

"I'm still hungry. Practice took it out of me."

Stevie smiles, shaking her head as she grabs a second fork from the drawer and hands it over to me. "You're lucky I have a soft spot for you."

Kissing her lips, I dig into my half.

It's been fun having Stevie around. Texting with her while I'm on the road. Make-out sessions when I'm home.

But that's it. Nothing more.

Every time I think we're finally going to take that next step, she puts the brakes on things. It's like a switch gets flipped and her walls go up.

When I ask her if everything is okay, she says it's fine.

I like what we have now, but I want more.

"How was work today?" I shovel a bite into my mouth and love the explosion of flavors on my tongue—the peppers and cheese and meat.

"Good. One of my regular clients was in and I always like working with her." Stevie wipes her mouth and grabs the water bottle and takes a sip. "How was practice?"

"Great. I think we're going to be looking good against the Black Diamonds."

"They're the best team right now, right?"

I kiss her. I can't help it. "I like it when you talk hockey."

A bright smile lights up her face. "So that means I was right?"

"Yes, as much as I hate to admit that they are the best team, you are correct."

"Yes." She pumps her fist. "Look at me. I'm the Knights' biggest fan."

I laugh. "I'll be sure to get that on a jersey for you if you ever come to a game."

"Does that mean I'll be invited sometime?"

"Do you want to come?" The thought of having her at a game excites me. I'd love for her to watch me in person, but I thought that would be too serious of a step.

"If you want me too, yeah."

"I mean, I don't want Caleb coming. I'd rather people not figure out I have a kid just yet."

Stevie gives me a warm smile. "You're a good dad, Bode."

"Thanks." I shy away from the attention, going back to the dish at hand. "Once we're done with this, you want to play some video games?"

"Video games? I don't know if you and I should play games together." Her blue eyes are sparkling. Leaning closer, I steal the bite off her fork. "Hey."

"Are you worried you're going to lose?"

Stevie sets her fork down and stands. "You'll have to show me, but let's do it."

Watching her walk into the living room, I can't help but admire her ass. God, what I wouldn't give to feel that with no barrier between us.

I shake that thought loose and follow her. There will be none of that tonight. Not until the woman who is driving me crazy decides she's ready.

"Do you need me to teach you the rules?"

She grabs the controller from my hand and drops down next to me while I pull the game up. One of my easier ones to ease her into it.

"I'm a quick learner. I should be able to get it."

"Want to make a bet on it?"

Stevie crosses her legs and looks at me. More like stares me down, but I love the fierce look in her gaze. "What do you have in mind?"

Oh, I have lots of things in mind, but I go with the easy one. "Another night of cooking together."

Stevie looks bewildered. "Seriously? That's what you want? A night of cooking?"

I nod. "It means another date with you."

She fights the smile, but it's useless. It splits her face wide open. "What a smooth talker you are."

"And if you win?"

"Can I wait and tell you?"

"I think that defeats the purpose of setting the bet before we play."

Stevie picks a character and I settle on my usual guy. Mario Kart is an easy one, and whoever wins, I'm happy that I get to spend the night with her.

The game starts and I take off, leaving her in my dust. Other characters keep bumping into her or dropping banana peels to send her spiraling.

"Hit the X button to block them." I let go of my controller to cover her hand with mine. "That'll get you around the other players to move up. And try and grab the health things on the road so you can attack others."

"Why are you helping me? Don't you want to win?"

Stevie's tongue is poking out of her mouth as her entire body turns with the controller. Fuck, if she isn't the cutest thing ever. She slides up to fourth place.

"I can help you and still play."

I have a solid lead as I kick my feet out onto the coffee table and steer my guy around the course. It's an easy one, a giant oval.

"Alright, well take this." I don't know what she does, but it sends a rocket flying at me.

"What the hell?" I try to recover but she goes zooming by me on the final lap. "How'd you do that?"

"I don't know. I did what you told me to do."

"Damn it." I pop up onto my knees, focusing on the game. I can see her pink car ahead of me as I dodge another player who flies by me. "C'mon, Bode. C'mon."

"I can see the finish line."

Stevie leans closer to the TV, but no matter what I fire at her, it's to no avail. She crosses in second place as I move down to fourth.

"Damn it."

"Yes!" She throws her arms up in victory. "I did it! Queen of the Road! Champion!"

It flashes for a second game, and I toss the controller next to me before tackling Stevie to the couch.

"Alright, Queen of the Road." I drop my elbows on either side of her head. "What is it you want for winning the bet?"

Stevie links her hands behind my neck and brings my face closer to hers. "I have a feeling it's something you might like."

"Oh yeah? What might that be?"

Her lips drift up my cheek, brushing the shell of my ear. A shudder racks my body.

"Take me upstairs, Bode."

"What?" That has me pulling back. "Are you sure?"

I don't know why I'm trying to talk her out of this, but after a month of nothing? I want to be sure this is what she wants.

"Yes."

One word. That's it.

Yes.

It's all I need to hear to start leading her upstairs.

Yes.

Chapter Nineteen

Y*es.*
One word and I'm running upstairs after Bode.

I've wanted this for a long time. Since the day Bode beat me in laser tag. But every time things start getting hot and heavy between us, I get nervous.

Things with guys always end once sex gets involved. I'm already in too deep with Bode and don't want to give up what we have.

What if I'm just another notch in his bedpost?

Why in the world did I say yes to this?

Seeing Bode standing at the top of the stairs, lust swirling in his dark eyes, reminds me why I wanted to say yes.

I take the last few stairs and stop.

"Are you having second thoughts?" There's a hesitation in Bode's voice. "We don't have to do this."

Closing the distance between us, I link my fingers with his.

"I'm scared," I confess.

Bode tucks a loose strand of hair behind my ear. "Of me?"

"No. Absolutely not. It's just…" I sigh, resting my free hand on his shirt-clad chest.

"Tell me. You can tell me anything, I promise."

I stare at my hand. It's easier than looking at him in the face. "We both have a past. You with all the women you've been with, and the few guys I've been with? They never made me feel great after sex."

"Stevie."

Bode says my name with such confidence that I have to close my eyes. I don't want this to go south before it even starts.

"Look at me." He puts his knuckle under my chin, tilting my head until my gaze meets his. "You have a past. I do too, although mine is longer. When I take you into my room, it's you and me. No one else. You are the only person that matters. No one else has ever been inside my sanctuary."

Bode leans closer, his lips ghosting my ear. "You, Stevie. I want you. No one else."

His confession has my body trembling. It has my own spilling from my lips. "I want you too."

"Then let me show you how much you mean to me."

Bode drags his nose along my neck, wrapping his arms around me and pulling me toward his room.

With each step, my fears of being cast to the side by this man dissipate and my desire amps up.

I want him.

Shutting the door behind me, Bode walks to the bed, grabbing the hem of his shirt and pulling it over his head. His jeans rest low on his hips, Vs leading into the waist of his boxer briefs.

"Like what you see?"

I nod, walking closer. "Yes."

"I really like that word."

Grabbing me around the hips, Bode throws me onto the bed and settles over me. Laughter bubbles out of me as he peppers my face with kisses.

When our mouths connect, they turn slow. Drugging.

I wrap my legs around him and feel his long, hard cock through his jeans. I gasp. "Holy shit."

Bode's lips kiss a path along my jaw, my neck, nibbling on the tender skin. "I plan to devour you, Stevie. Every inch of this body. I want to show you just how much I care about you."

"Do it. Please."

Warm, open-mouthed kisses suck on my exposed neck as he peels open the buttons of my blouse. Goose bumps erupt on my skin.

"I've been dreaming of this moment," Bode whispers against my breast.

Pulling the cup of my bra down, he takes my nipple between his teeth.

"Gah."

It's the smallest of touches, but it lights me up from the inside out.

"You like that?"

"Yes. More."

Strong, callused fingers work with deft skill as they undo the button on my jeans. Peeling me out of them, he tosses them behind him.

He rocks back onto his heels. "Where to start?" He taps one finger to his lip.

"Here." I swipe a finger over the band of my underwear.

"And how would you like me, hmm? My mouth? Fingers? My cock?"

I nod. "Yes. All of the above."

Grabbing the material in one hand, Bode rips it off in one go. "I have been dreaming of this pussy." He sinks one finger inside of me and I almost combust. "Thinking how warm and delicious it would be. I want to see you come as I eat you out."

Bode's brown eyes lock with mine as he closes his mouth over my folds. I don't look away, even as I arch off the bed.

Every lick, every suck, every brush of his fingers strumming my clit is a tease. A slow torment as he keeps working me over just enough but not tipping me over the edge.

"Make me come, Bode."

He pushes another finger inside, spreading them open. "I don't think you've asked nicely."

"How nicely do I need to ask?" I whine.

Bode shifts back, wiping his mouth. "Hmm. I think I need to hear another please. Maybe some begging."

He swipes a finger through my wetness before sucking it off his finger. Why is it so hot seeing Bode's obvious pleasure for me?

"I'm not hearing anything."

I throw my head back onto the bed. "Please, Bode. I want to come."

"Where?"

"Your tongue. Fingers. I'm not picky."

A cocky smile spreads across his face. "I am. And you are going to come for the first time on my tongue."

He seals his mouth over me and works his tongue inside of me.

"Oh!"

Combing my fingers into Bode's hair, I hold on for dear life as his eyes tell me to come.

One more quirk of his finger and I explode. Heat

floods my body as a feeling unlike anything I've ever felt fills every crack.

"Bode. Bode!"

His fingers squeeze my thigh as he guides me through the overwhelming pleasure. When it feels like I've come back into my body, Bode's grin is one I'll always remember.

"Do you realize how sexy you are, Stevie? How fucking amazing you taste? Unreal."

My heart feels like it's going to burst out of me at his words. I don't know why I waited this long to have sex with Bode. Of course he would make me feel nothing but cherished.

"I think it's time you feel how you made me feel."

Bode fishes into his nightstand and pulls out a condom. While he sheds the rest of his clothes, I slip out of my blouse and bra. Heavy-lidded eyes rake over my body as I take in his cock.

Long, hard, and thick, it's already leaking. And I can't wait to feel it inside me.

"Are you going to make me come again?" I squirm as Bode's heavy weight settles on top of my now naked body.

"You want to come on my cock? Think you can handle it?"

"Why don't you find out?" I waggle my eyebrows.

Bode doesn't need another word as he slowly guides himself inside me. Slow inch by slow inch. It's tight, but he lets me adjust before he thrusts all the way in.

"I'm ready."

We breathe each other in as he pumps his hips. I widen my legs to cradle him as he keeps moving. With every thrust, he picks up his pace. It hits a place deep inside of me that I haven't felt touched in years. A place where cobwebs are growing.

My pussy is squeezing him to within an inch of its life. I'm so close to coming again that I dig my heels into his ass to keep him moving.

His head drops closers to mine, that floppy hair of his falling over his eyes.

"Bode…"

Too many emotions are swimming through me. Bode is waking up parts of me that I never knew existed.

"You going to come? I'm not coming until I feel you come on my dick."

"I…I…" I shatter. Every part of my body becomes unglued into a thousand pieces of rainbows and stars. My nails dig into Bode's back as I cling to him. It's like I'm floating into a new universe.

I've never felt so free. So incredible.

Bode's release slams into him, filling the condom.

"Fuck!" he growls out.

Bode's hot body collapses on top of me. I hug him to me, running my fingers along his back, feeling every notch in his spine.

A happy contentedness settles inside me as we lie here together. No words need to be said as Bode kisses my shoulder.

"Rest up, Stevie. Because if the first time is that good, I plan on making you come all night long."

Chapter Twenty

STEVIE

"**D**o you have to work today?"

Bode's head pops over the couch. It's been a lazy morning here. Since he doesn't have to play until this afternoon, we spent what little time there was before Caleb woke up in bed.

It's still dark outside, a fog lingering.

I shake my head, adjusting Caleb in my lap. He's playing with a toy while watching some show that Marcus and Harper recommended to us. "Not today. I have the day off."

Bode's head moves closer. "Want to take Caleb apple picking?"

I turn toward him ever so slightly. My eyes adjust at how close he is. "Can he even eat apples?"

"Not a whole one. I'd have to cook it for him, and make sure there's no skin so it's easier for him."

That pulls a smile from me. Well, a bigger smile. Because how can you have the world's cutest human on your lap and not smile?

"What's that face for?" Bode asks, leaping over the

back of the couch and settling next to me. Every inch of him lines up to me and warmth radiates off him. Even through the sweatshirt of his I'm wearing, I feel it.

"Nothing. It's sweet you know these things."

Bode shrugs, taking Caleb into his arms. Caleb's hands go to his face, trying to find purchase. "Well, as his dad, I need to figure this shit out."

"I think you're doing a pretty good job." I press a kiss to his cheek.

He rests his head against the back of the couch, staring at me. Emotions bubble up inside me. How can looking at someone make me feel so warm and fuzzy inside?

I don't think I've ever felt anything like this. Sure, I've dated guys in the past, but one look from them never made me feel so happy.

"Honestly? I'm glad I have you and our grandmas helping. I don't know if I'd be able to do it without you guys."

I stroke Caleb's soft cheek. His focus is on the toy in hand, ignoring the two of us. "I think you're doing better than you think. You don't need us."

"Don't even say that," Bode tells me. "Besides, Gran is supposed to watch him tonight."

"What are you three up to this morning?" Nan walks into the living room with Eve behind her.

Bode stands, hefting Caleb up into his arms. "I've got my game this afternoon, but we're going to go to the apple orchard this morning. Want to come?"

"Apple picking with him? Oh, Deb, we have to put him in the pumpkins and take a picture." His grandma's eyes light up. Eve takes him from Bode's arms and heads upstairs. "We'll get him dressed. Be ready to go in twenty minutes."

They're gone before we can get another word in.

"What, that's it?" Bode stares down at me, a smile playing on his face.

I jump up to meet him and wrap my arms around his waist, resting my chin in the center of his chest. "We better get moving. We don't want to keep them waiting."

"You know," Bode starts, his eyes dark, "I was going to shower before we left."

"Imagine that. I was planning on doing that too."

"Should we maybe save time and do it together?"

"I don't know how much time we'll be saving…" I trail off. Grabbing Bode's hand, I put a sashay in my hips and lead him upstairs.

Bode grabs me around the waist and throws me over his shoulder. "Better make it fast, Stevie, because we only have twenty minutes, and you know they won't wait for us."

"REALLY. You'd think we didn't give you two enough time," Nan moans as we all hop out of the car.

The gravel parking lot is crowded. Even with low clouds hanging in the sky threatening rain, it's still busy.

"Twenty minutes is not enough time to get two adults and a baby ready to go," Bode tells them.

"One adult," Eve corrects him. "We took care of Caleb."

"Yeah, yeah." Bode gets the baby carrier out of the trunk and secures it to his chest before putting Caleb in it. "At least you put him in a cute outfit."

The orange, red, and yellow striped romper has leaves and pumpkins all over it. Paired with a mini jean jacket and tennis shoes, he looks adorable. His legs are kicking in front of him as he faces out toward the orchard. A bucket hat sits on his head in case it rains.

"He'll be the cutest kid out here."

A wooden house with a red roof welcomes us to the Bradford Family Farms. The smell of leaves hangs heavy in the air. Tractors roll out toward fields filled with pumpkins. Wooden crates filled to the brim with apples sit on either side of the walkway.

"Want to start picking apples and then we can head toward the fields?" Bode asks.

Sunglasses cover his eyes, and a worn, plain black hat covers his hair. You would never know he plays for the Knights with the gray hoodie and plaid jacket he's wearing. I threw on the first thing I could find that was clean—a black sweatshirt, olive jacket, and leggings. There was no use in putting on a hat when I swept my wet hair up into a bun.

By the time I was dressed and covered my face in basic makeup, we were getting yelled at.

Wet bun it was.

"Now, you know Caleb can't eat apples, right?" his gran points out.

"You'd think I'd never done this before. Almost like she doesn't trust me." Bode ignores her and speaks at me, heading toward a wagon to start loading up with apples.

"What? It's not like you've ever raised a kid before. Just making sure."

I grab Bode's free hand, and we wander through the rows of trees. Leaves are crunching under our feet as we stop every so often to peruse the fruit.

"These look good." Bode grabs some of the apples sitting on the higher branches.

"You know this is why we always need a tall person around," Eve says.

"So I can pick apples for you?" Bode smiles at her.

I love the relationship the two of them have. They always poke fun at one another, but you can feel the love they have for each other.

"Hey, I don't want grubby little kid hands on my apples."

I burst out laughing and grab a few red ones that look good. "We'll have to make sure we get some green ones too. I can make some apple crisp when we get home."

"Does everyone get this?" Nan asks.

"Only the people who are picking apples," Bode points out.

So far, neither of our grandmas have picked apples. They're walking behind pointing out which trees look good and oohing and ahhing over Caleb.

"Look,"—Eve reaches up to pick a ripe piece of fruit— "I get apple crisp now."

I shake my head at her antics. "I promise, everyone will get apple crisp when we get home. As long as you promise to save some for Bode when he gets home."

"At least someone is on my side." Bode presses a kiss onto the crown of my head.

"Oh, Deb. Grab a picture." Eve waves at her and passes her phone over.

Bode tugs me close and before I can look at them and smile, Caleb starts making noises at the apple in his hand and I laugh. Based on the reaction of the two of them, it's a good photo.

"Look how cute you all look together." Nan holds the phone out so we can see.

I suck in a breath. Caleb is looking at the apple with a confused face, not quite sure what he's supposed to do with it, I'm laughing at him, and Bode? Well, he's looking at the two of us like we're the best things in his world.

"Would you look at that?" he whispers so only I can hear him.

"I love it." It's the only thing I can say. Because in reality, saying we look like a family would be too much.

When I moved in, the last thing I expected was to fall for Bode. I didn't need to get involved with anyone. I was trying to lick my wounds and recover from my ex kicking me out.

Falling for Bode and his kid? That was unexpected to say the least.

Learning how to trust myself again has been a process. With Bode, I feel safe to do it. He never pushes me to do anything I don't want to do.

The man who says he only ever worried about himself isn't that same guy. Every day spent with him, I see how selfless he is. With Caleb. With me. With our grandmas.

He's the first thing I think about in the morning and the last at night.

Could I…could I be falling in love with Bode?

No. It's way too soon. We've only been together a few weeks. Having sex the last few days.

Right?

"You alright, sweetheart?" Nan links her arm through mine as we follow Bode, Caleb, and Eve through the rows of trees.

"I'm good. Just thinking."

"About how cute all of you are together?"

"Nan," I moan.

Leave it to her to know. She's always been able to read me like a book, but I've never been one to hide my emotions away.

"What? I'm only saying what I can see with my own peepers. Even I don't need glasses to see how much you two are into each other."

"You know you sound like you're in high school when you say that, right?"

Nan laughs. "Well, someone has to be the fun one around here."

"Hey. Are you saying we're not fun?" I goad her. "I'll have you know today is a perfectly fun day."

She stops and stares me down. Her brown eyes are wide under her round glasses. "A fun family day. You don't go out and have enough fun on your own."

"Yeah, yeah." I take Caleb from Bode as we settle onto a picnic bench and he goes to get us some drinks. "Why don't you and Eve go see if there's any pumpkins we can take home."

She gives me the side-eye. "I see what you're trying to do."

"Get rid of you so we can be done with this conversation? Maybe I should be more subtle."

"Okay." Nan stops Eve and heads back toward the pumpkin patch.

"Did you get the same lecture?" Bode asks, sitting next to me and setting a warm glass of apple cider in front of me.

"About how we're no fun?"

Bode laughs. "I don't think they'd understand, but this is the most fun I've had in years."

"Me too."

"Good." Bode clinks his glass to mine. "This is the kind of fun I want to keep having."

"Same."

Because sitting by Bode's side in the cool fall air, life finally feels like it's looking up. Like I clawed my way out from rock bottom and the sun is finally shining again.

The perfect day.

Chapter Twenty-One

BODE

"Hell yeah!" Marcus jumps on top of me as the horn blares through the arena. The fans are on their feet as we celebrate a goal late in the third.

The grin on my face spreads as I skate by the bench, bumping gloves with my teammates. "Way to go, Adams!" Coach yells as I skate back to my starting position for the puck drop.

Damn. That one really felt good. We're leading Dallas 4-1 now with only a few minutes left. The home crowd doesn't sit for the remainder of the game as the energy flows down onto the ice.

Even with Dallas pulling their goalie, they can't get another goal. Defending our end of the ice, I send the puck flying toward their zone and land it in the center of their net.

The red light flashes across the ice as I skate toward the bench.

"That's what I like to see." Coach Andrews claps me on the back as I grab my water bottle and take a swig.

"Maybe next time you'll go for the hat trick." Noah laughs, elbowing me in the side.

"Sorry to disappoint."

By the time the final horn sounds, we've put the game away, 5-1. We'll be heading into the All-Star break soon, and going on a winning streak feels fucking amazing.

Plus, if we keep winning, it'll make it that much easier to secure a spot in the playoffs. No one is saying it, but we're all thinking about it.

We don't want to jinx ourselves just yet.

"You want to grab a quick drink before heading home?" Marcus asks, as I come back to my stall after talking to the press and a quick shower. "Harper is taking the kids over to my mom's tonight so we can have the evening to ourselves."

My gut reaction is to say no. I want to go home and hang out with Stevie and Caleb. The idea of going out no longer holds the same appeal that it once did.

But now? I wouldn't mind going out to celebrate a great win with the guys.

"Sure, why not?"

"Wow. Way to sound excited," Jasper chides.

I not so subtly flip him off before I grab my suit jacket and toss it over my arm. "Hey, Caleb comes first now."

Marcus claps me on the back as we all stand and start to head out. "He should. But it doesn't mean you can't hang out with your teammates."

"I guess so."

The guys give me shit all the way out of the arena. Broadway is packed with people as we make the short walk to The Sin Bin. Seeing as how it's our usual spot after home games, fans tend to come here. But Chad, the owner, always reserves space in the back room just for us.

We wave at him as we duck into the back room and order a round from the waiting server.

"First round is on me," I tell the guys.

"Damn. Killer game and buying drinks? Someone's in a good mood," Jasper says.

I stretch my legs out, crossing my arms over my chest. "What can I say? It was a fucking great game."

And after this I get to go home to my kid and Stevie? Yeah, it's been a good day for sure.

"Sorry for the delay, guys; it's been a busy night." Chad drops off our drinks. "But I can't complain. When you win, they come out in droves."

"Guess we need to keep winning then," Graham says, raising his glass in cheers.

"I'll drink to that."

I sip on the beer as the guys rehash the game. It's something we always do together when we go out. We started doing it when we were losing as a way to try and figure out how to improve.

Now? It's nice to see that we're doing well.

Graham elbows me in the side as the guys keep talking. "How are things with Caleb going?"

"Great." I can't help the smile that spreads across my face. "I love seeing his personality start to come through."

"Think you've got a little hockey player on your hands?"

I shrug a shoulder. "Way too soon to tell. I'm just happy when he's happy."

"Such a dad thing to say."

I point a finger at him. "Hey, just wait until you and Noah have kids. You'll be just as sappy."

"Not until we've done a few more things together," Graham tells me.

"Do I even want to know?" I quirk a brow at him, taking another drink of my beer.

"I meant winning a cup together, you dick. Head out of the gutter."

I throw my hands up. "Hey, you took it there, not me."

"That's a change for you," he says.

"Dick." I flip him off.

"Aww, are you two being mean to each other?" Noah goads.

"Just talking about when you two have kids," I tell him.

"Not before we win a cup," Noah says, rapping his knuckles on the table.

"Sounds good to me." I laugh, looking around for our server. Based on the noise filtering back here, the bar is packed. "I'm going to go grab a water. Anyone need anything?"

Heads shake as I head into the packed main room of the bar. It's wall-to-wall bodies. It makes me thankful we have our own space to relax after the game.

Squeezing my way through the people, I flag down one of the bartenders pulling beers.

"What can I get you, Bode?"

"Just a water." I pull out my wallet and drop a twenty into the tip jar.

"Hey there."

I drop my eyes to the brunette standing next to me. "Hi."

"Bode, right?"

"Yeah."

Based on how she's looking at me, she knows exactly who I am.

"You want to get out of here? Go somewhere a bit quieter?"

"Can't. Sorry."

Had this been before Caleb came into my life, I might have taken her up on her offer. I am a completely different person than who I was before. I like who I am now. I feel more settled. More at peace.

Who would have thought?

"What, so you're too good for me, but not for her?" she sneers.

"I'm sorry, what?"

What in the world is this woman talking about?

"You can date some rando, but now you have standards? She's not even pretty. Bet she doesn't know how to get you off."

I take a deep breath before I go off on this woman. I've interacted with her for all of ten seconds. The last thing I need is to be in the press for being a jackass. Even if she crossed the line into classless conversation.

"I'm sorry, I have to go."

She calls out after me, but I can't hear a word she's saying over the noise.

I make a point to never search for myself online. I don't want to know what the outside world is saying about me.

But this? This I have to know. Especially if it affects Stevie.

I pull up the browser on the phone and type my name in the search bar.

There's a grainy photo of Stevie and me at the laser tag place. Thank God it's not from when we were apple picking. I don't know what I would do if Caleb's face was out there for the world to see.

Looking at the website hockeybunnies.com—I can at least rest easy that it's not on the main news channels. Only some blog.

"You okay?" Marcus asks when I walk back into the room.

"I'm good." I drop some money onto the table for our drinks. "Listen, Gran called and Caleb is getting fussy, so I'll see you guys tomorrow."

The lie slips out easily as I wave goodbye. After the encounter with that woman, I'm out of sorts, and now, all I want to do is get home to Stevie.

Thankfully, most of the game traffic has cleared out and it makes for a quick drive. It gives me just enough time to sort through my thoughts before I get home. I don't want to worry Stevie about this when there's nothing to worry about.

"Oh, well, if it isn't Mr. Playmaker himself." Stevie is waiting for me on the couch. I breathe a sigh of relief. Who knew one look at someone would settle all the intrusive thoughts going on inside?

"Where's Gran? I thought she was watching Caleb tonight?" I ignore her comment. *Fucking nickname.*

"She went to bed. I told her I'd wait up for the player of the game."

The house is quiet. It's just her waiting to greet me. I flop down onto the couch next to her. She's wearing an oversized Knights hoodie—mine—and a pair of skin-tight biking shorts.

"They didn't pull out that ridiculous nickname again, did they?" I groan.

She nods, resting her hand on my chest and giving me a kiss. "I'm not going to lie, I like it. Mr. Playmaker."

"Stop it." I fist a hand in her shirt and pull her over onto my lap.

"Oh, I'd like to see these plays you've got." She waggles her eyebrows at me. Her hair flows down over her shoulders. I want to wrap my fist around it and pound into her.

"Would you now?" I fire back at her. "I didn't think you'd be impressed with them."

She drags a finger down my chest. "You don't need to do anything more to impress me. But…"

"Yes?" I drag my nose along her neck, inhaling that sweet scent of hers. One that I've found I've quickly become addicted to.

"Remember my secret talent?" Stevie asks. Her knees shift, brushing against the outside of my thigh.

"Secret talent?" I ask.

"You remember. I always win at board games."

"That's not a secret talent," I tell her, bursting out into laughter. "It's all luck."

"Hey. It is. I'm great at board games." She pokes at my chest. "And tonight, I am going to prove it to you."

"Oh yeah?"

She nods. "We're going to play a game of Sorry. No bets, because I don't want you to lose after winning your game tonight."

"Wow." I shift her off my lap and we both stand. "You are really feeling yourself, aren't you?"

Stevie walks backward, grabbing the game off the coffee table and heading toward the kitchen table.

"Yes. And I am going to prove to you just how good I am."

Grabbing two waters from the fridge, I take a seat at the table and adjust the board so my four yellow pieces are in front of me. "Remind me how to play?"

Stevie gives me a cocky smile as she explains the rules. I could listen to her talk all day. I don't know how I got so lucky to have this woman land on my doorstep, but I'm glad it was her and not anyone else.

"Think you got it?" Stevie asks.

"I got it."

We start, and Stevie lets me go first. No luck getting out, but she does on her first draw.

Taking turns, she moves around the board, all of her pieces getting out while I have only one out.

"I don't understand how you're so good at this."

Stevie sips her water. "Because I'm amazing at board games."

"It's all luck!" I tell her, throwing down a card that doesn't let me move. "How are you so lucky?"

She waggles her eyebrows at me as she pulls her card to get another piece into the safe zone.

"Sorry. I'm just good."

I give her a playful glare as I take my next turn, finally getting another piece out. Not that it's going to do me any good at this point. Unless she draws every terrible card in the deck, I'm going to lose.

In Sorry.

A board game that Caleb could probably play. Well, maybe not Caleb...but still.

She moves another piece home and I move a few places up.

"It's unfair that you're almost home and I still have two pieces waiting to get out."

She smirks at me and before she can tell me how good she is, I plant a kiss on her lips. Hopefully one to distract her.

Not good enough.

She shoves me away. "Nice try. I'm not losing."

"Okay, Miss Playmaker."

She winks at me. "I'll take that nickname happily."

"Of course you would."

Stevie grabs another card and her last piece moves into home.

"Fuck. Are you serious?" I stare at the board. "I really don't get how you're so good."

Leaning across the board, a big smile is spread across her face. "Do you want to play again?"

"Hell no."

"Want to do something else?" The way she says it, that slight teasing, has my cock thickening in my sweats. Especially when she sips her water with a knowing look on her face.

"Like?" I lean over the board, dropping my hands on either side of her. Up close, I can see the tiny dark blue flecks in her eyes. The way they widen slightly at my nearness.

"I can make you feel better after losing." Her breath ghosts my mouth.

"You can?" I hold her chin between my fingers.

She breaks the contact, standing up and kneeling between my legs.

"I can. Now, hands behind the chair."

Holy fuck. I don't know where this Stevie came from, but I do as commanded.

Because I can't wait to see what she does.

Chapter Twenty-Two

STEVIE

Kneeling between Bode's knees makes me feel powerful. In command.

His dick is hard and his tongue darts out to lick his lips.

Yes.

I love that I am the one making him feel like this.

Bode ditched his suit jacket and tie, but is still in the black pants and white button-down. With deft fingers, I ignore the bulge in his pants and slowly undo the buttons of his shirt.

"Christ, Stevie. Really?"

"I'm in charge."

He throws his head back as I expose each inch of skin of his chest. I take my time, memorizing every inch of him. The shape of his pecs. The way he sucks in a breath as I brush over his nipples. Tracing each and every one of his multiple abs.

"Do you know how hard it is to sit here and not touch you?" Bode growls.

Glancing down, I'm pleased to see the tent in his pants has gotten even bigger.

Pressing up onto my knees, I capture his lips in a quick, hot kiss. "You want your cock in my mouth? Is that it?"

"Fuck, Stevie. Do it."

"No."

"No?" he questions.

"Not yet."

Rocking back on my heels, I grab the hem of Bode's sweatshirt and pull it up and over my head. His eyes go to my bare chest, where my nipples are diamond hard.

"This is just mean."

"What can I say? I like teasing you."

I press open-mouthed kisses to every inch of his chest. My hands explore him as I do what I want. Right now, Bode is my plaything and I plan to torment him the way he's done to me.

His hips thrust off the chair, but I don't give in to him. I push the shirt off his shoulders and stride around the chair to knot the material around his hands.

"If you are going to try to move things along, I am going to have to tie you up."

"Damn it."

Standing half naked in front of him, I smirk down at him. "I like seeing you like this."

I drag a finger down his chest, watching the shudder rack his body.

"Meanwhile, all I want is for you to be sucking me."

"Tsk, tsk. Maybe I should just go and do something while you wait."

A growl rips deep from his throat. The sound of it has me not wanting to wait any longer. His need is potent. I finally unzip his pants, and his dick pops out. Long, thick, and already dripping. "I see someone is needy."

"So needy," he parrots back. "Please, Stevie. Please."

"Please what? What do you want?"

"Your mouth. Do what you said. Take my cock in your mouth."

I drag my tongue over the bulbous head, tasting his salty precum. "Mmm. I knew you would taste amazing."

His cock is too big to fit inside my mouth. I slip my hand into my shorts, pushing my fingers inside my own wet pussy. Coating them, I take them out and slowly start to jack Bode off.

"Holy fuck, Stevie. Oh God."

I can't take him to the back of my throat, but my hand and mouth work in tandem. My nails dig into his thigh as I let my tongue slide down the throbbing vein on his underside.

I pour attention on him as I twist my hand and suck him off. Every sound he makes hits my ears and goes straight to my pussy. I'm dripping wet.

Apparently, driving this sexy man wild turns me on. When I look up at him, his head is tossed back in pleasure and his glistening chest is heaving. His body is tense, and feeling his cock swell in my mouth, I pull off him.

"Don't come."

"What?" From the look on Bode's face, he's in a daze.

Reaching into his pocket, I fish out his wallet and grab the condom. I press a kiss to the top of his impossibly hard dick and roll it down.

"As much as I want you to come in my mouth, I want to feel you inside of me."

Not wasting any more time, I toss my shorts and underwear to the side and sit on top of him, sliding down slowly.

"Fucking finally."

I trail kisses up his neck. Kissing. Nibbling. Sucking. "Do you know how good you feel filling me up? The way you fit inside of me? I love it, Bode."

"Your pussy is so damn perfect, I want to cry."

I don't even know if he hears what he's saying as I move over him. The slow roll of my hips amps up my pleasure. Bode is close to the breaking point. I make his pleasure my own as I move my mouth over his. I want everything this man will give me.

His mouth closes over my nipple, tugging on it. I cry out in pleasure.

"Bode—"

Before I can say another word, Bode pulls his arms out of his restraints and lifts me off him. Turning me, he pushes my chest down onto the table where game pieces go flying as he thrusts back inside.

"Oh!"

"Perfect." Bode's chest covers my back as he moves inside me. He tugs my earlobe between his teeth, flicking his tongue over the sensitive flesh. He lifts my knee onto the table to open me up. "You were made for me, Stevie. Your pussy? It's heaven. I could die happy right now."

Bode reaches around me and strums my clit. "Keep doing that."

"I'm so close, babe. I need you to come."

"Harder, then. I want to feel it tomorrow."

The only sound that can be heard is the slapping of skin against skin. Each thrust reaches a place deep inside me that has me ready to explode.

"Fuck, Stevie. Fuck. I'm going to—"

He can't finish the sentence before he's coming with me. He empties his release into the condom and it tips me over the cliff.

Falling into the abyss with Bode is indescribable.

He's shouting. I'm shouting. I have never felt like this before. So lost in bliss, that I don't know which way is up.

I can't move. I know I should, but I'm not ready to

break the moment. I want to bask in Bode for as long as possible.

I don't know how much time passes before Bode pulls out of me. I stay put until his warmth surrounds me and he lifts me into his arms.

"C'mon, champ. I think you might need a recovery period before we do that again."

"Play Sorry and me beat you?"

He smacks my ass as he throws me over his shoulder and jogs up the stairs.

"If that's what you want to do, I might have to make you come again."

"You better."

And that he does. All night long.

Chapter Twenty-Three

BODE

"What about this?" Stevie holds up a hanger. The matching set has brown striped pants with a giraffe on the sweater.

"I don't know. Brown doesn't seem like Caleb's color."

"You do realize how cute he'll look in this, right?" Stevie rolls her eyes at me and holds it up to the baby in question. He's sitting in the baby seat in the cart as we wheel him around the store. "I'm getting it for him and you can't stop me."

"Caleb is already spoiled enough. He doesn't need more things."

Stevie crosses her arms and looks from me to the shopping cart. "Bode. You cannot say he is spoiled and doesn't need more things when this cart is overflowing with things for him."

"I'm not spoiling him," I defend. "He needs these things for winter."

Caleb's brown eyes flit between the two of us. Like he can't decide what is going on and who is right.

"You have two coats for him. Why does he need two coats?"

Stevie cocks an eyebrow at me and holds both of them up.

"What if he spills on one?"

"He's a baby. Of course he's going to spill on it. Wipe it up and move on."

"But he'd look good in both of them. How can I choose?"

"He's a baby. Babies look cute in everything. Even if you think brown isn't his color."

Glancing down at the baby in question, I have to admit Stevie isn't wrong. On this outing today, I put Caleb in joggers, a little Knights sweatshirt, and a beanie to match. With the weather starting to turn cold, I wanted to make sure he was warm. He's been playing with a stuffed hockey stick the whole time we've been here.

"Fine." I grab the black coat from her hand and find the rack to hang it back up. "But if he destroys his coat and we don't have one for him, I'm blaming you."

She stops me before I can push the cart any farther away and tugs me back. Her blue eyes are playful. "Does that mean you're going to punish me?"

My eyes dart around, making sure there isn't anyone near us. After that woman approached me at the bar, I can't be too careful. "You cannot say things like that in the middle of a store, Stephanie."

She rolls her eyes at my use of her full name, then waggles her eyebrows at me. "Maybe I meant to say it…"

Burying my face in her neck, I press a chaste kiss to her warm skin. "There will be a lot of spanking tonight."

I can feel her shudder all the way to my toes. Until Caleb lets out a cry. Turning to face him, I laugh at his bottom lip sticking out.

"Are you sad we're not paying you attention?" Stevie blows a raspberry on his cheek, which earns her a happy squeal.

"If I cry and pout like that, will I get attention?"

She shakes her head. "No. It's only for the cute ones."

Damn. I laugh as I follow her to the front of the store. Who knew shopping for baby things could be so fun?

The checkout area is busy as we make our way to one of the lines. I give my hat a nervous tug down. I don't want to spend the rest of the afternoon fielding picture or autograph requests. I want to pay, pack up the car, and go home and hang out with Stevie and Caleb.

The ideal day.

I smile as we start to unload the cart. The cashier gushes over how cute Caleb is as she checks us out. Thankfully, we manage to make it out of the store without anyone spotting me. I load up the car while Stevie buckles Caleb into his car seat.

You couldn't wipe the grin off my face the entire way home if you tried. How can shopping make me feel so good?

I've come to learn it's the little things that matter. I always used to give Marcus grief over him wanting to spend so much time with Harper and his kids, but now I understand it. I crave it more than anything. More than hockey even.

These low-key days with Stevie and Caleb are everything.

"You are quiet," Stevie tells me as I pull into the driveway and shut the engine off.

"Just thinking."

"Yeah? What about?"

Unbuckling herself, she pauses as I lean across the

console. Sunglasses hide her eyes. There's an easy smile on her lips.

"You. Caleb. Today."

"And?"

"I'm happy."

She gives me a quick peck on the lips. "I am too."

My heart swells at hearing that.

How did I get so lucky to find someone like Stevie? That our lives managed to combust at the exact same time and we crossed paths?

Getting out of the truck, I start to unload the bags from the back. Caleb is snoring softly. "If you want to put him to sleep in my room, we can unpack everything in his."

Stevie nods, unhooking the car seat and carrying him inside.

I whistle as I head straight to Caleb's room to start pulling everything out of bags. Half of the clothes in the closet go into tubs to be returned to Marcus and Harper. The others that he grew out of, I'll donate.

The room aired out nicely after I had it painted a light blue. With new furniture delivered, I'm ready to make this room his.

"We really did some damage today, didn't we?" Stevie asks, wrapping her arms around me.

"Did he go down okay?"

Pressing onto her toes, she kisses my cheek. "Didn't make a peep."

She grabs a bag and starts taking the hangers off and tossing the clothes into the laundry basket. Something else I learned. You always have to wash new baby things.

Who knew?

"Where do you want the pictures?"

Moving on from the clothes, Stevie holds up the new prints.

"Above the crib."

We work together like we've been doing this our whole lives. I hang the new art while she arranges the books and blankets we bought.

Before I know it, cries can be heard from my room.

"I'll go get him," Stevie tells me.

"Thanks. I'll do one last sweep to make sure everything is cleaned up."

I don't want any stray things going into his mouth.

I lean against the wall and slide down to the floor, surveying our hard work as Stevie walks in and takes a seat next to me. Caleb is still waking up from his nap.

"This feels more like Caleb," she tells me.

"It does."

He doesn't care, but I do. His room before felt like a quick fix to get it ready for him. Now that his personality is shining through, I wanted a place that was more his.

The late-afternoon sun streams into the room, reflecting off the blue walls. Watercolor pictures of animals playing hockey hang above his crib. The oversized chair was replaced with a rocking chair that has a soft baby blanket thrown across it along with Caleb's favorite stuffie.

A new stack of books sits on his dresser, my favorite being the *ABCs of Hockey*.

Stevie is bouncing Caleb on her lap, and emotions bubble up inside me. Seeing her with my son brings up emotions I never thought I would experience. I was fine being a lone wolf, doing life on my own. I didn't want to rely on anyone.

Maybe it was because I never met anyone like Stevie.

I don't have to be anyone but myself when I'm with her. She doesn't care that I'm a hockey player or about my past. I'm not putting on a front. I never thought I'd be the kind to stay in every night, but I want to. I'd rather spend all my time playing board games with Stevie and Caleb than go out to bars. Being with Stevie makes me feel more whole than I've ever been in my life.

How can one person heal all my broken parts?

How can I say those three little words to her when I've never said them before? It feels too heavy. Like if I say them, I'll mess up everything we have together.

"Hey." I rub a hand down Stevie's back. She turns to me, a happy smile on her face. "I'm glad you're here."

"I am too."

Maybe that's all I need to say for now. Until I figure out how exactly to confess my feelings to her.

Chapter Twenty-Four

BODE

"Do we have enough time?"

Gran and Deb came home shortly after we finished his room, and they offered to take Caleb for a walk. There was no way I was going to refuse that offer, and now I want to make every use of this short window the two of us have together.

"Stevie, there will never be enough time in the world to be with you." This woman only walked into my life a few short months ago, but I'm not sure any amount of time with her will be enough. I want every second with Stevie that I can get.

Pressing kisses to her neck, I steer her into my room and kick the door shut. My hands are groping for purchase as I pull her in closer.

I thrust my hips forward, letting her feel exactly what she does to me.

"You drive me wild, Stevie. I've never felt like this before." It's as close to an admission of what I feel for her as I'll get right now.

"Bode," Stevie purrs.

"What do you want?"

"You."

Spinning her in my arms, I push her onto the bed and stare down at her. Her pupils are wide with lust. Desire.

Capturing her mouth with mine, I claim her lips with the kiss to end all kisses. Each moan and whimper from her I lap up. It drives me forward, leaning over her and resting her on the bed.

I change my pace, slowing my tongue as I relish her taste. Stevie gives over complete control to me. Her nails dig into my neck, urging me on. Every stroke of her tongue against mine has me rolling my hips into her.

Rocking back onto my heels, I slowly peel Stevie's shirt up and over her head. Her breasts are heaving. I lick my way along the supple skin, loving how she's a writhing mess beneath me.

I bite her nipple, visible through the satin material of her bra.

"Do that again," she moans.

"You like that?" I repeat the motion, nibbling on her soft skin.

"Yes. So much yes."

Peering up at her, her eyes are shut, hand pushed through her hair. Her lips are swollen from my kisses.

I can't wait to see how debauched she will be once I'm done with her.

"You have no idea how much I like seeing you like this. That it's me making you feel so out of control."

"I love it when you touch me, Bode. I've never felt like this before."

I smile against the soft fabric of her pants as I trail a path of kisses to her hipbone. "Only me?"

"Only you."

"Good. Because I am going to show you just how much

I love making you feel this way. How much I love your body."

Stevie sinks her fingers into my hair and twists. I look up at her, gazing down at me with eyes so dark, I can barely see the hints of blue there.

"Give me everything, Bode. I need it."

"Whatever you want, Stevie, you'll get it. I'll give you everything."

With deft fingers, I undo the button of her jeans and pull the material down and over her legs. Tossing them behind me, I settle on my knees between her own spread ones. A wet spot grows on the red cotton of her underwear.

"Is this how wet you are for me?" I ask, rubbing the tip of my finger over the wet material.

"Yes. You always make me feel like this."

"How do I make you feel?"

Shuffling down the bed, I pull the underwear off and immediately devour her pussy.

"Gah!" she shouts.

Pushing her knees wider, I open her up to me.

"Tell me. Tell me how I make you feel," I demand.

I tease her clit, brushing my nose against it as I delve my tongue in her warm wetness.

"Desired."

"More."

I nip and suck on her, letting her coat my lips.

"Cared for."

"Go on."

"On edge." I sink one finger inside, curling it toward me. "Yes! Oh, Bode. So good. Right there."

I continue my ministrations, working her over and soaking up every sound she makes. My cock is rock-hard, ready to thrust inside her and make her come, but not yet.

I want her taste on my lips when I make her scream my name again.

"Are you going to come for me like a good little girl?" I suck her clit between my lips, rolling my tongue over it. "Are you going to let me know how I make you feel when you come?"

"Bode!" Stevie squeezes her thighs against my head, her release taking over her body. "Yes! Yes! Yes!"

I smile as I drink up every drop of her orgasm.

"Fuck." I wipe my mouth. "You taste so fucking good."

Stevie is blissed out, eyes closed as her chest heaves with deep breaths.

"You are the most perfect thing I've ever seen." I can't stop the words from spilling out of my mouth. But they're true.

Stevie responds by linking her hands behind my neck and taking my lips in a searing kiss. I'm greedy. Hungry for each glide of her tongue against mine.

How can each time with her get better and better?

I can't imagine a time when I don't want Stevie. When I don't crave her with every cell of my being. It's not just the sex. I feel like myself when I'm with her. Like I don't have to put on a show—be Bode the hockey player who oozes swagger.

I'm just Bode. The insecure guy who has no idea what he's doing with his life and hopes he's not fucking everything up.

"I need you, Bode," Stevie whispers against my lips.

Flipping her onto her stomach, I reach across the bed to pull out a strip of condoms.

Shucking my pants and boxers, I throw my T-shirt off and roll the rubber over my dick. Seeing this woman laid out for me has me needing to take a few breaths to settle myself.

"What's taking so long?" Stevie wiggles her ass, and that has me covering her body with mine.

"You want my cock? Is that it?"

"You know I do."

Pressing her thighs apart with my knees, I slide my dick between her ass, letting her feel just what she does to me.

"Hold on." Taking her hands, I rest them against the headboard. "This won't be gentle."

"I don't want gentle. I want you to make me scream."

Wrapping my fist into her hair, I drop my mouth to her ear. Her skin is hot beneath mine.

"There will be no screaming today, otherwise I'm going to have to punish you. Understand?"

"Mmm."

I slap her ass. "Understand?"

She wiggles back against me, soaking my condom-clad cock with her wetness. "What if I want you to punish me?"

"Oh, Stevie. There will be a time for that." I squeeze her reddening ass cheeks together. "I promise. But I want to enjoy that. A slow torture."

"And you won't enjoy this?"

"Oh, no. I will. But I need to come now."

Unsnapping her bra, I toss it to the floor and push her down in the sheets. I look at her, feeling like I'm in a dream.

A dream I never knew I had. It's like there's something inside her that calls to me and only me.

I slide into her, letting her warmth take over. "So fucking good."

"Hard, Bode. I need it hard."

"Whatever you want," I tell her as I thrust my hips.

My moves are punishing. Hard and fast. Each jack of my hips has my blood sizzling for this woman. Leaning over her, I cover her body with mine.

"Do you know how good your pussy feels?" I ask her.

"Tell me." She turns her head back and I capture her mouth in a heated kiss.

"I love how I can feel how wet I make you. Like every squeeze of my cock is urging me on. Like it was made just for you."

"Bode," she purrs. "I love how good you feel inside me. Your cock is magic."

I can't help my triumphant smile as I go faster. Just when I think I can't wait any longer, Stevie shouts, exploding around me.

"Thank fuck." Grasping her hips, I thrust once, twice more before emptying into the condom.

I let the blinding heat pulse through me as she chokes my cock with her pussy. I don't know if an orgasm has ever felt this good. Stevie's release pulled mine out of me.

Reaching around her, I keep her close to me as we both come down from our highs. She's whispering nonsense as she buries her head in the pillow.

"That's it. Hold on."

"How is it so good?" Stevie's hair sticks to her face as I pull out and drop down beside her, taking care of the condom.

"I don't know, but I'll do it again to find out."

She peeks one eye open at me. "I'm sure that will be a hardship for you."

"A burden I must bear."

She burrows into my side and I relish these last few minutes of peace we have. Her fingers trace my abs as I drag my fingers up and down her arm.

I love this woman, and I will do whatever it takes to keep her here.

Chapter Twenty-Five

STEVIE

I'm nervous. I wish I weren't, but I am. Nerves and excitement have been competing in my belly all day. I've never been to a hockey game before. Now, my first ever is one where I'm dating one of the players? Are we dating? We haven't put a name on what we're doing, but it feels like we're dating. Actually, a lot more than just dating with the way I'm feeling about him.

I want to be with him all the time. I love getting to be with him, and I've never felt more at peace than I do when I'm with him. Like Bode calms me in a way I never knew I needed.

Parking my car, I take a deep breath and try to push down all these emotions. Grabbing my bag, I step out and shove the key in the lock—not that anyone would try to steal this old thing in a parking lot full of much nicer cars —then head inside, following the groups of people. Bode told me exactly where to go.

The doors automatically open to an elaborate lobby. It's business-like, but everyone is decked out in Knights gear.

An older woman is sitting at a desk. "Hi there. Bode Adams left a pass for me."

"Name, please?"

"Stephanie Campbell."

She taps away on her tablet before looking up at me. Grabbing a pass hanging on a lanyard, she hands it over. "Here you are, ma'am. If you'll take the elevator at the end of the hall up to floor three, they will show you to the suite."

"Thank you."

I smile at her as I follow her directions. I blend into the crowd with the people here. Bode got me a red Knights ball cap to wear. Paired with a black bomber jacket and jeans, I felt cute when I left the house. Now I'm wondering if I should have splurged on a jersey. Because when the elevator doors open, I'm swept into a sea of them. Every player is represented. It's overwhelming. The sound of the crowd erupts. I have no idea what is going on, but I find a desk in the center of the room.

I planned my arrival as close to the start time as I could. I'm nervous being here on my own.

"Hi. I'm looking for suite…" I look down at my badge. "Seventeen."

The man with red hair smiles at me. "Yes. If you follow this hallway down, it's halfway down on the right."

"Thank you."

When Bode said he got me a pass to the game, I didn't think it'd be in a suite. I would have been just fine in the nosebleed seats.

But as I find the suite in question, my nerves are ready to jump out of my throat.

What am I even doing here? Groups of people are lingering with drinks in hand. Chafing dishes hold all sorts of food. The back wall holds a counter with a sink and various drinks. Grabbing a seltzer, I stand in the corner.

It seems like everyone here knows each other. It's one of those times I'm thrust back to that girl who worries about everyone else liking her. Some days I feel like a confident woman, and others, I'm that girl struggling with a mother who didn't care.

"Hi." A woman with stunning looks and blonde hair walks over to me. "Are you Bode's guest?"

"Is it that obvious that I'm new here?"

"Bode told Marcus he invited someone, so he told me to look out for you."

I smile at the kind woman. "Yeah, I'm Stevie."

"Harper." She holds her hand out and I shake it. "C'mon. The game is about to start. Have you ever been to a game before?"

I follow her out to the seats and drop down next to her. "First time."

"You'll love it. The games are fun, especially now that the team is doing so well."

The game starts and it's hard to follow the puck up here. It's fast-paced, moving from one end of the ice to the other.

"Is the game always so fast?"

Harper nods. "It was hard to follow at first, but you get used to it."

"Yeah?" I ask, sipping from my drink.

She nods. "I've been a fan since I was in college. Fell for Marcus the first time I saw him. I love watching him play. It's hard to describe, but you'll know it when you feel it."

I try to find Bode on the ice, but it's hard from up here. "I can imagine it's fun watching them. I did try to look up a few things, and I've been watching on TV so I wouldn't be a complete newbie."

"Well, if you need help, let me know."

It's nice to have made a friend. It seems like all I do lately is work and hang out with Bode. Not that I'm complaining, but with Cressy all loved up, it's nice to meet new people.

When did making friends as an adult become so hard?

"Mom, can we have dessert?" Two girls run up to Harper.

"These are my girls, Sam and Sadie. Jamie, our son, is at home with Grandma tonight. He cannot sit still during games."

"Hi." I smile at the twin girls standing near Harper.

"Hi," they answer in unison.

She glances at her watch. "Did you eat the broccoli and carrots I gave you?"

"All of them."

"Then yes, you can have a cookie. But just one!" she shouts as they run back up into the room. "I swear, those two have a sweet tooth now that I can't control."

I laugh. "Well, at least we don't have to worry about that with Caleb."

Harper shifts toward me as the game continues in front of us. "How are things going with him?"

Her voice drops so people can't overhear us. I know Bode is trying to keep everything quiet about him. He doesn't want Caleb in the spotlight, which I can appreciate.

"He's great. I've never been around kids much, but he has so much personality."

"I'm glad things are going well for him. Bode looked so freaked out that day. I didn't think he was going to last a week."

Pride swells in my chest at how well he's doing. Even that stressful first day I arrived, Bode has been nothing but the best father to Caleb. He always puts him first. I love the relationship they have. Seeing the way Caleb lights up at Bode?

It makes me want to be a permanent part of their lives.

"He loves being his dad," I answer instead. Harper is a mother. She knows all this already.

Action picks up and the crowd starts yelling. Bode is taking off down the ice. He's all alone with only the goalie of the opposing team to stop him. Making a few quick moves, moves I can't name, he puts the puck in the net.

"Yes!" I jump up and cheer with the rest of the stands. Excitement courses through me as the goal is replayed on the jumbotron.

Damn. Bode made that look easy. His skill was on full display as he sent the puck flying.

"See what I mean?" Harper nudges my side.

"What?" I lean closer, trying to hear her over the crowd noise as play resumes.

"Watching your guy play. It's an incredible feeling."
"Yeah."

I can't describe it, but I know exactly what she means.

Harper and I chat during the entire game. I talk with her daughters about their school and activities. By the time the final horn sounds, Nashville has won 2-1.

"Okay, you have to come to another game," Harper tells me as we head toward the postgame suite. "This was the most fun I've had all season."

"Really?" I grab my hair and pull it all to one side over my shoulder. A nervous tic.

"Yes." She leans close and whispers, "Some of these women are so bland to talk to and we have nothing in common. It's like talking to cardboard."

I try not to laugh as we step out of the elevator. "I'll see if Bode can make it happen."

"If not, I'm claiming you as mine. Because I want you here."

"Thanks, Harper. I had a great time with you too."

She smiles at me as we walk down the cement tunnel lined with red carpet. Plaques line the wall next to banners from sponsors, along with pictures of what look like old team lineups, if I had to guess. Harper guides me to a room filled with people. Beige walls and a few couches grace the room. TVs hang in each corner, showing highlights from the game and player interviews.

There's a door opposite us that some players have started coming out of. The girls spot Marcus and run to him.

Bode is right behind him.

"Have a good night." Harper gives me a hug as she goes to greet her husband.

When Bode spots me, he saunters over to me.

"Hey."

"Hi." I tuck my hands into my jeans pockets as he spins my hat backward.

"How was the game? Did you have fun?"

I nod. "It was great. Thanks for having Harper look out for me. It was nice getting to know her."

"I'm glad."

I grab his tie, smoothing it across his chest. "You looked good out there."

Bode moves closer. "Only good?"

"Well. I have nothing else to compare it to, so I'm going to have to come back, I think, to make an educated assessment."

Bode beams at me. God, I love his smile. That dimple that always pops? I love it. "I think I can arrange that."

"Want to go out and celebrate your win?" I ask. "That goal was something else."

Bode drops his hands on my hips and leans close to whisper in my ear. "I was thinking we could go home and watch a movie?"

"Sounds perfect to me."

Chapter Twenty-Six

BODE

"You have the blanket?"

"Yes." The oversized blanket is laid out on the couch as I dim the living room lights. The baby monitor sits on the table with a sleeping baby filling the screen. "Popcorn done?"

"Yes. What do you want to drink?" Stevie calls out from the kitchen.

"Water is fine."

The sounds of cabinet doors opening and closing echo around the room.

"I hope you're ready for this."

"I'm ready to see what you've been going on and on about."

"I have not been going on and on," Stevie tells me, walking into the living room. "If you don't love this, I don't want to know."

It's been a while since Stevie and I started this thing, and I'm finding it harder and harder to keep my feelings to myself.

Especially after inviting her to the game. It felt like a

very public pronouncement of my feelings toward her. Even if it was only the guys who saw us together.

Every time I want to tell her I love her, it's like the words get stuck in my mouth. I turn into a bumbling idiot, and I end up asking her what she wants for dinner. Even if it's ten o'clock at night.

The smell of butter wafts through the living room as Stevie sets the bowl of popcorn on the table with two glasses of water.

"You don't?" I ask, holding my arm out to her for her to lie next to me. I pull the soft blanket over us and let her burrow into me.

She shakes her head. "No. This is one of my favorite movies, and I will not let you ruin it for me."

"Hey. Who says I'm going to ruin it?"

She rolls her eyes and cues the movie. "You're a man and we're watching a period romance film. You wouldn't be the first."

"We'll see about that."

Stevie starts the movie as I grab the popcorn bowl and take a handful. I'll be the first to admit, this isn't my kind of movie. But I'll be damned if I let Stevie know that. If she asks, I love it.

When the camera pans to all the daughters, my jaw drops.

"I'm glad I only have Caleb; I couldn't imagine that. Five daughters? Yikes."

Stevie throws a piece of popcorn at me. "Shh!"

"What? I'm only saying I can relate to him. That's a lot of kids."

"It was more common then. Now shush."

Stevie quiets me by turning the volume up. I smile as I pull the blanket over us and cozy up into the couch.

"This is my favorite part. Watch."

Stevie turns up the volume, cuddling farther into my side. I squeeze her close, letting her sweet perfume wash over me.

"Wasn't that great?" she sighs.

"They didn't say anything."

"You missed it?" She sounds affronted. "How could you miss it?"

"You can't turn the volume up and expect me to see something. I was listening."

"Watch," Stevie goads me as she turns back to the TV. "Watch his hand."

It's a flex after he helps her into the carriage. It's the most subtle of moves. Blink and you miss it. Stevie pauses it and turns to me.

"It's my favorite part of the movie. He loves her so much, even the briefest of touches is too much."

I can easily say I know the feeling—the overwhelming awareness of being so in love with someone that you have no idea how to handle it.

This movie is hitting a little too close to home for me. I can relate to everything this Darcy fellow is going through.

"So this Darcy guy…he's already in love with her?"

Stevie nods and starts the movie again. "Yes. Can't you tell? He conveys so much love with just one gesture."

"Will they end up together?"

She smacks me in the chest. "I can't tell you that. You need to watch."

I smile at her before pulling her into my side. My fingers rub up and down her sweatshirt-clad shoulder.

As the movie goes on, I find I'm more and more invested. This poor schmuck is so in love with Elizabeth. Is he going to tell her? I don't know if I could stand it to think of these two not being in love.

"You have bewitched me, body and soul."

Damn. I guess when Darcy figures shit out, he goes for it. Maybe I could take a page from his playbook.

"Yes! C'mon. Say yes, Elizabeth." I rub my hands together, leaning toward the screen. "How could anyone possibly say no to that confession?"

"Watch." Stevie shushes me once again, but when they kiss, I can't help the emotions that take over.

Tears wet my eyes as they ride off into the sunset.

"Fuck. That was good."

Stevie shuts it off and turns to face me.

"Wait. Are you…are you crying?" Stevie leans back, locking eyes with me.

"What? No." I grab the empty bowl of popcorn and head to the kitchen, discreetly wiping my eyes.

"You are!" Stevie follows me, hopping onto the counter next to the sink. "You loved it, didn't you?"

"Okay, fine." I set my hands on my hips. "What's not to love? The poor bastard is so in love he doesn't know what to do about it and almost loses her."

Something I can very easily relate to.

Stevie claps her hands together, holding them over her heart. "And that confession? It gets me every time. Darcy is the perfect man."

"Oh, he is, is he?"

Grabbing her knees, I push them apart and close the distance between the two of us.

"I mean, it's the truth."

I give her a devious smile. "I mean, he kind of is. He knows exactly what to say to make Elizabeth come back to him."

Stevie links her hands behind my neck and pulls me in for a kiss. Slow. Sweet. Languid.

I'm addicted to her kisses.

"I mean, you're also pretty great."

"I'm no Darcy…"

"Eh, not everyone can be."

I give her one last kiss before putting the popcorn bowl and glasses in the sink. Darkness has swallowed us. The only light is the soft glow of the living room lights, casting long shadows.

"Hey. Would you have any interest in bringing Caleb to the game next weekend? I figure an afternoon game won't throw off his schedule," I ask, changing the subject. I don't need to keep thinking about Darcy and his love confessions.

That's a problem for future Bode.

"Really?"

I sweep Stevie's long blonde hair behind her shoulder. "Yeah. I want you to come see me play again, and I want Caleb to be there too."

"Even though he won't be able to remember any of it?"

I drop my hand onto the elegant column of her neck, rubbing my thumb along the vein there. "I will. I want my son at the game."

Stevie's smile is hesitant. "I mean, if you're sure."

I capture her lips in an easy kiss. "Yes. I want you there. Both of you."

"We'll be there." Stevie hops off the counter and walks backward toward the stairs. "Now, care to join me upstairs?"

I nod. "Be there in a minute."

I watch her go, eating up the view of her disappearing up the stairs. I am in over my head with this woman. I don't know how I fell so hard, but I did.

I need to grow a pair of balls. Be like Darcy and confess to Stevie how I feel.

I mean, the guy made it look easy.

How hard can it be?

Chapter Twenty-Seven

STEVIE

"**A**re you excited to see Daddy play?"

Caleb looks up at me with big brown eyes. Tiny headphones are secured around his ears, protecting him. He doesn't understand a word I'm saying, but his face is happy.

He definitely takes after his father.

Going in through a separate entrance, I follow the path I took the last time I was here.

I adjust Caleb's jersey, one that says "Daddy," as we take the elevator up. Bode bought him one with his last name on the back, but Eve thought it would be a fun surprise for Bode after the game.

"Good afternoon. Can I help you find where you're going?"

I smile at the older gentleman. "Hi. I'm headed to suite seventeen, but is there any place we can store his stroller?"

He beams at me. "Ahh, yes. Right this way."

I push the stroller after him.

"There's some space back here," he starts, pointing to

the small entryway I didn't notice the first time I was here. "You can leave it here so it's out of the way."

"Thank you so much."

Voices filter out of the suite into the hall.

Before too long, I won't be able to hold him. He's growing like a weed and is getting heavy.

"Stevie," Harper greets me, "I'm so happy you could make it tonight."

"Thanks." I adjust Caleb on my hip, who now has a fistful of my hair in his mouth. "It's nice to see you again."

Having a familiar face here makes it less awkward. Having walked in by myself the last time I was here, it feels different taking Caleb.

I'm not his mom, but I feel protective of him.

Harper gives me a one-armed hug, thanks to the screaming toddler on her arm. "Sorry about him."

"Is he okay?"

Harper waves me off. "He's fine. The girls went to the bathroom with their Gigi and he got mad that he couldn't go."

"Ahh. Well, at least we don't have to worry about that with this one."

Harper smiles at him. "How's he doing?"

"You mean how is Bode doing with him?"

She shrugs and leads me farther into the suite. "I mean, you said it, not me."

Food of all kinds is spread out across the counter. Pasta salad. Sliders. Mac and cheese. Hot dogs. All of it smells delicious. Tubs of ice hold soda and various drinks.

"Pretty sure that Bode is Caleb's favorite person."

Harper eyes me. "From the looks of it, you're also right up there."

"Stop it."

"What? I'm only telling you what I see with my own

eyes." Harper piles some veggies onto a plate and bites down on a carrot with a hearty crunch. "He's never invited anyone to a game, and now this is your second time here."

I hide the blush on my face by getting a few things out of my bag for Caleb to eat.

"Grab a plate and come sit with me."

I do as Harper says and get both of us settled as the players come onto the ice. It's nice being in the suite with additional chairs.

Caleb can't sit still with Jamie running around, so I set him down so the two of them can play.

"It'll be nice when Caleb gets bigger so these two can have playdates," Harper says.

I take a bite of one of the sliders and wipe my hands on my napkin. I'm sporting my own Adams jersey and can't wait for Bode to see me in it.

Another surprise for today.

"Maybe we can have you guys over for dinner one night. The kids can all play together."

Harper beams. "I would love that. It's hard to find people that know what this life is like."

"I'm still learning the ropes."

She reaches over and clutches my hand. "You're doing great. Don't let anyone scare you off."

Sam and Sadie come running inside, and the minute they spot Caleb, they start cooing over him.

"Can we play with him?" Sam asks.

"Of course," I tell her.

Harper nods toward the seats out front, and we leave the kids to entertain themselves as the pregame festivities start.

"Aren't the girls going to come watch the game?"

She shrugs. "They might, but now that you brought Caleb, I think they'll play with him. They love babies."

I laugh, sipping on the hard seltzer I grabbed for myself. "Does that mean it's time for another baby for the two of you?"

"Marcus wants one, but we had Jamie so fast after we renewed our vows, that I want to enjoy a little more time with my husband."

"I can completely understand that."

She elbows me in the side. "Does that mean you're enjoying your time with Bode?"

"Very much so."

"We are going to need to have a girls' night so I can get the scoop."

Harper gives me a knowing smile as others start to take their seats.

Girls' night and a couples' date night with Harper?

I feel like I belong here now.

As the anthems start, I grab Caleb so he can watch the puck drop. His eyes are wide as he takes in the flashing lights. Bode's face flashes across the screen and I start cheering.

"Go, Daddy!" I hold up his little fist.

"Wait, do that again. Bode will want a picture," Harper tells me.

I let her take a picture as the puck drops.

We take our seats and chat throughout the game. We cheer on the team as they score, and the girls take Caleb back with them to play. They are more interested in him than the game.

Marcus scores with an assist from Bode, and the two of us yell and cheer. Pittsburgh matches our goal easily, but after that, it's all Knights.

Bode ends the first period with a goal, and then starts the second period with another.

"Maybe he's trying to impress someone." Harper winks at me.

My cheeks heat at watching Bode. The camera cuts to him and *wow*. I don't think I've ever seen Bode look so sexy. He exudes happiness as he skates to the bench.

I did not fully appreciate Bode skating last time. Or maybe I was paying more attention to the game.

It has heat swirling through me. I can see the appeal of falling for a hockey player. The strength and skill they have out there is unmatched.

I grab Caleb for the third period, and I'm glad I did. Because right as I'm snapping a photo of him watching the game, Bode scores.

His third of the night.

The crowd goes wild as hats start landing on the ice.

"Why is everyone throwing their hats on the ice?" I ask Harper.

"He got a hat trick. Three goals."

"Oh, I knew that. I didn't know they threw hats. Good to know."

"It's okay. I wasn't a hockey fan until Marcus."

"I can honestly say I agree. Well, Bode. Not Marcus."

She smiles at me. "They'd turn anyone into fans."

I laugh as someone from the team skates onto the ice to collect all the hats. Pittsburgh scores once more, but it's too little, too late.

Nashville gets the easy 6-2 win.

"Want to come see the guys?" Harper asks, gathering up her purse and jacket. Her jean jacket has Marcus's number on the back with a few patches of the Knights sewn on.

"Sure. Cute jacket, by the way."

"Maybe I'll help you make one if you want."

Grabbing our things, I smile as I put Caleb in the stroller. "Maybe our next girls' night."

The two of us exchange numbers as we take the elevators down to the family suite. Guys from the team start to come out, and when I see Bode, I know the minute he spots us.

Having lifted Caleb into my arms, he sees the jersey he's wearing. His face lights up as he jogs over to us.

"How in the world did you get this?" he asks, taking Caleb from me and pressing a chaste kiss to my lips.

"Eve helped me with it. Thought it would be a fun surprise."

He smooths it over Caleb's belly and takes the headphones off his ears.

"Did you have fun, Caleb? It was your first hockey game." Caleb smacks him in the face, loving the attention. "How'd he do?"

"Great. Sam and Sadie played with him throughout the game. Jamie kept taking his toy, but he thought it was hilarious. He's going to sleep well tonight."

"You know what that means?" Bode waggles his eyebrows at me.

I slap a hand over his mouth. "You cannot say that around the baby."

"I said nothing," Bode mumbles against my hand. "You're the one that made it dirty."

"Oh, and that wasn't your intention?" I cock an eyebrow at him.

"I was going to say we could go home, put this little guy to bed, and then play a mean game of Sorry."

Crossing my arms, I stare up at him. His brown eyes are playful. "That's what you had in mind? Sorry?"

Bode leans down and gives me a sweet kiss, but not

before a tiny fist smacks my cheek. "See? Even Caleb is calling your bluff."

Bode laughs before wrapping his arm around my shoulders and pulling me in close. "C'mon. Let's get out of here. I'm ready to get home with my two favorite people."

A blush heats my face at his words.

His two favorite people?

Things are going well, but I didn't think they were going this well. Something I'm learning about Bode is that he plays it close to the chest. But inside that chest is a heart of gold. Something he doesn't show to just anyone.

I consider myself lucky that I get to see this side of him.

Playful.

Sweet.

Kind.

Caring.

And oh so sexy.

I only hope I'm the only person that gets to see this side of him.

Because I want Bode Adams all to myself.

Chapter Twenty-Eight

BODE

DAX

Have you seen the news?

BODE

What news?

DAX

About you and Stevie

Fuck. What happened?

NOAH

I thought we decided to wait and tell him at practice?

DAX

I thought we said we were going to tell him before

GRAHAM

Do I need to send you a screenshot of our text?

You guys have a group text without me?
Fuck off

MARCUS

It's only because we were discussing what
to do

JASPER

Or in this case, what not to do, Dax

Will someone tell me what's going on?

JASPER

There's a photo of you, Stevie, and Caleb
after the game

DAX

It looks like you're dating

We are dating

NOAH

Well, if you didn't want word getting out
about you two, you did a bad job of it

GRAHAM

And there's a lot of questions about Caleb

Fuck

What are they saying about him?

MARCUS

It's mostly about you and Stevie

JASPER

But the comments are nasty

DAX

Which is why I thought he should know
before practice

I appreciate you telling me

NOAH

No names were dropped, but there's a lot
of speculation

JASPER

I wouldn't go reading it if I were you

Like that's going to happen

MARCUS

We're here if you need us

DAX

What he said

NOAH

Ditto

GRAHAM

Ditto? Really?

NOAH

What? I agree. It means the same thing

JASPER

Ignore them. We're all here for you if you
need anything

Bode: Really not making me feel better
about this

JASPER

Sorry. But you should know we've got
your back

I appreciate it

Thanks guys

A lead weight settles in my stomach. An article about me, Stevie, and Caleb? Fuck. That is the last thing I want. I thought it would be okay to have Stevie bring him to a game. I wanted Caleb there. I know he won't remember the game, but I'll never forget having him here.

Seeing his happy face after the game, in a daddy jersey? I don't think I'll ever forget that moment. Sharing it with Stevie? It made it that much better.

All those good feelings are wiped away as I type my name into the search bar and wait for the results to come up.

Holy shit. Article after article comes up. There's a grainy photo from the game of the three of us outside of the arena last night. I'm pushing the stroller and Stevie is looking up at me.

Fuck. Fuck. *Fuck.*

I thought we were being careful. I know every way out of the rink and took the one that fans don't know about.

But someone saw us and snapped a photo.

Opening my social media accounts, my messages are flooded. I don't think I've ever seen so many comments before.

Women sad that I'm off the market.

Others calling Stevie a home-wrecker. Not sure how that term applies, but it doesn't make it hurt any less.

A few are even saying their kids are mine and photos are sent. A can of worms has been opened. I wish I could stuff it all back inside and rewind the last twelve hours.

I have to tell Stevie. I can't let her be bombarded like this. I left her sleeping in my bed.

It was the perfect evening. We ordered takeout, played with Caleb, had dinner with our grandmas, and then spent all night wrapped up in each other.

"Everything okay?" Stevie stretches out next to me.

It's still dark. Caleb is still fast asleep after his big day out, but the buzzing of my phone woke me up.

I flip on the bedside lamp, the soft light bouncing around the room.

"Can we talk?"

A look of dread washes over her face as she sits up. "Is everything okay?"

"Between us? Yes," I clarify. "But there's a photo circulating of us from the game last night."

"What? How? I thought we were in a restricted area?"

I shake my head. "It's when we were leaving. I thought we were okay, but turns out—"

"Oh my God. Is Caleb's face out there? Do they know he's your son?"

This has me grabbing her by the shoulders and pulling her in for a hug. I bury my face in her neck and breathe in her sweet scent, letting it sink into me and settle my nerves.

Her concern for Caleb is why I'm so far gone for Stevie, it's not even funny.

"It's blurry, but his face is there. They haven't figured out his name, or yours, but it's only a matter of time."

"Are you okay?" Her warm hands rest on my back, her fingers rubbing soothing circles on the exposed skin there.

"Not really. People are being cruel. The comments are…well, I don't even want to share them."

Stevie pulls back, cupping my cheeks. Her eyes are sad and angry, mirroring my own. "What can I do?"

I kiss the beating pulse of her wrist. "Can you not go looking for it? I don't want you seeing some of the comments out there."

"Done."

"Really? Just like that?"

"If it's as bad as you say, I don't need to."

"It's bad." I sit back, checking my phone to see that Caleb is still asleep. "The worst part of all of this is him getting dragged into it. He didn't ask for his dad to be a hockey star."

"We'll do everything we can to protect him. Me, Nan, Eve. You're not alone in this, Bode."

"I love you."

I can't help it. I can't keep the words in any longer.

"You what?" Stevie looks stunned.

"I didn't want to blurt it out like this, but it's true. I love you, Stevie. The way you care for not only me, but Caleb? You're one of the only people in my life who doesn't care that I play hockey. I love you, Stevie, and I wish I could protect you from this, but I can't, and for that, I'm sorry."

"Stop it." She places her hand over my mouth. "Bode, I love you. I love Caleb. As much as you think this is your fault, it's not. Whoever decided to out us? It's their fault. They can say whatever they want about us, but we know the truth."

I smile against her hand and pull it off. "You love me?"

She runs her hands through my messy hair, rubbing my cheek. "Of course I do. You're the only person who has never made me feel less than because of my past. I feel my most authentic and beautiful with you, Bode, and I never want to lose this feeling."

"I love you, Stevie. Even if you think you're really good at board games, when it's just luck."

"Hey." She smacks my chest. "I am good."

I nod, smirking at her as I push her back into the soft pillows of the bed. "Okay, babe."

"See if I play any more games with you."

I laugh, easing the tension that's gathered in my shoulders.

"This is why I love you."

"Because I beat you at board games?"

I kiss her, soft and sweet. Maybe the best kiss of my life. "Among other things."

Stevie sighs, pulling me in close. "So, what do we do?"

We.

I'm not alone in this. It's the two of us.

"I'll work with the PR team to get ahead of it, but it might get worse before it gets better."

"Then it's a good thing we'll have each other to weather the storm together."

"God, I love you."

Now that I've said it, I can't hold it back. I want to shower Stevie in all the love I never got. To let her feel it every single day.

Whatever happens, come what may.

We'll handle it together.

Chapter Twenty-Nine

STEVIE

If there's one thing I love about my job, it's working in one of the most calming places.

The zen-like music is always playing in the halls to better the experience for our guests. Lavender and bergamot perfumes the air. Bamboo lights hang from the ceiling, casting long shadows through the halls.

Heading to the front desk, I smile at the receptionist. "Hey, Becky. Do you have my list of appointments for the day?"

"Umm, no."

"What? I'm booked solid all day."

Tuesdays are my day off, but I checked my schedule on Monday before leaving. Back-to-back bookings all day.

She gives me a saccharine smile. "Sorry. You had a lot of cancellations. Not just today."

"Are you serious? Did they say why?"

"Something about your personal life and getting in the way of doing your job."

"My—"

Oh, shit. The blood drains from my face as I rush back

to the locker room. Throwing open the door, I don't pay anyone in here any attention as I grab for my phone. Pulling open social media, I have hundreds of notifications. Even more messages.

Bile rises in my throat.

I shouldn't. I *know* I shouldn't, but I do it anyway. I tap on my messages and read them. I told Bode I wouldn't read the comments, but it looks like they figured out it was me in that picture.

"How dare you ruin a family. You should be ashamed of yourself!"

"Bode was in love with me, you slut"

"Get stuffed, ho"

"You only wish Bode loved you. He'll never love anyone as ugly as you."

HOLY SHIT. I barely make it to the trash can before I'm getting sick. There are hundreds of messages like that. One after the other.

No wonder everyone canceled their appointments today. Grabbing a piece of gum from my purse, I chew on it as I see more comments on my posts.

I can't imagine what they're saying everywhere else.

Bode said it might get worse before it gets better, but this? I never pictured it'd be this bad.

How can people be so vile?

"Hey. You okay?" Cressy's voice has me looking to her.

"No." There's no use pretending. I doubt I look okay right now.

"What's wrong?"

She sits next to me and drops a soothing hand on me. Handing over my phone, I watch in horror as her face changes.

"Where the hell do these people get off treating a stranger like this? You did nothing wrong."

"I don't even know how they found me. I mean, why do they care?"

Cressy scoffs. "I mean, these people are delusional if they think they have a chance with Bode. To call you… ouch, I can't even repeat this one."

I squeeze my eyes closed, trying to stop the tears from coming. "Well, seeing as how I have no appointments today, I'm going to use a sick day and go home."

"Do you want me to come with you?" she asks.

I shake my head, taking my phone back from her. "No. I'd rather be alone."

Cressy wraps me in a hug. "You don't have to be if you don't want to."

"Right now, I do."

"Just remember, I love you and there are people who love you. Don't take what the people are saying to heart."

"Love you too."

"Cressy, your next client is here." Becky peeks her head into the door before glancing at me and scurrying out.

"And that's my cue." Standing, I grab my coat and purse and duck out without anyone noticing me.

Unlocking my car, I get in but don't start it. People are bustling about in the outdoor shopping center where the spa is located. The sun is shining on this cold day.

How is it no one tells you that the most normal of days is when your life will get turned topsy-turvy?

I can't believe this has happened. I can't believe they figured out who I am. Sighing, I grab my phone and shoot off a text to Bode.

STEVIE

How on earth did they figure out this was me?

BODE

I don't know.

Stevie, I don't even know what to say

I'm so sorry

It's not your fault

How bad is it?

Do you want me to break my promise to you that I wouldn't go looking?

Now that they know it's you, you can't avoid it

How bad?

Bad

Seems I'm the most hated woman in Nashville

I love you, if that helps

A little

I'm headed home now

Wait, why?

Apparently people don't want a terrible person giving them a facial

Shit

The team is issuing a statement

I doubt it will help

Look, go home, have some wine

Scream, shout. Maybe beat our grandmas
in a game of Sorry.

I'll see you when I get home from practice,
okay?

And maybe I can beat you in a game

And then I'll make you forget all your
worries

I'm holding you to that

Whatever it takes

I'm here for you

I love you, Stevie

I love you too

FEELING SOMEWHAT BETTER after talking to Bode, I start the car and head home. There's no use in focusing on all the bad. I need to push it out of my head and hope the statement from the team will let things settle down.

Fingers crossed.

Chapter Thirty

STEVIE

"Is it weird I'm nervous for tonight?"

"Why are you nervous?" Bode wraps his arms around my waist and tugs me back into his chest. It's my favorite place, being surrounded in his warmth.

"I've never hung out with the guys before."

"You've hung out with Harper."

"That was at the game," I correct. "We had something to talk about and it made it easier. I don't know the guys."

Bode presses a kiss to my neck. "Then talk hockey. You won't get them to shut up."

"Easy for you to say. I want them to like me."

Spinning me in his arms, Bode drops his hands on either side of me, caging me in. "Trust me, they will."

"You sound so confident."

"Because you're an easy person to like."

The softness on his face, the look of adoration, makes me weak in the knees. Who knew Bode Adams could make me feel so many things?

He's been my rock this week. Through the barrage of comments and harassment I've gotten, I couldn't have made it through without him. And with the endless cancellations at work, I've been twiddling my thumbs at the spa.

With no clients, there's no money coming in.

It sucks, plain and simple.

Before I can say anything else, the front door opens and pattering feet carry themselves into the kitchen.

"Hi, Bode!" One of Marcus and Harper's daughters comes running around the island. "Where's Caleb?"

"What am I? Chopped liver?" Bode laughs.

"We want to play with him. We liked making him laugh."

"He's in the living room," I tell them. "C'mon."

Spinning her around by the shoulder, I lead her into the living room. Caleb is sitting in the pack 'n play we set up for him. "You've got some people that want to see you."

Lifting him out, she immediately starts cooing over him. "He's so cute."

The guys filter in through the door, as Harper and the rest of her kids walk toward us.

"Hey, Stevie."

"Hi. I'm glad you guys could come over tonight."

"Even if we ended up bringing all the guys?" she says.

I laugh. "Bode didn't want to leave them out."

Harper shakes her head as Sadie comes over to us. "Can we all play together?"

"Yes." She sets Jamie down on the floor next to Caleb. Now that he is crawling, we have baby gates set up in the living room to try and keep him contained. But with him pulling himself up, it's only a matter of time before he starts walking. "Just make sure they don't put anything they shouldn't in their mouths."

She nods and drops down onto the ground next to her siblings and Caleb. Watching Caleb's fascination with them is sweet. It was like this at the hockey game.

Harper links her arm through mine and pulls me into the kitchen. "I cannot wait until they are old enough to babysit."

Looking behind me, the two of them are pulling toys out and holding them out to the boys. "Think they'd want to come babysit Caleb?"

"Gladly."

All of the guys are in the kitchen, and my nerves are kicking in. These guys are like Bode's second family.

"I think it's time I officially introduce you all to Stevie."

"It's nice to actually meet you." Jasper sticks his hand out for me to shake. "Can't believe you like this idiot."

"Hey!" Bode scoffs.

I cough in my arm to cover my laugh. "I think he's a keeper."

"Jasper, be nice," Dax chides, pulling the cork on the bottle of wine and pouring a few glasses. "You don't want to scare her away."

"Like you saying that is any better?" Noah smacks him on the back of his head. "It's nice to meet you."

"Nice to meet you too."

"I'm Noah's boyfriend, Graham."

"Hi."

I don't think I've ever been surrounded by so many attractive men before, but none of them hold a candle to Bode.

"I hope you guys want burgers, because I bought enough to feed a small army," Bode tells them.

"Sounds good to me," Jasper tells him, grabbing a beer from the fridge. I take one of the wine glasses from Dax.

"Why don't you go start dinner?" Harper asks them.

"Can't we visit before?" Marcus asks.

"No," she says matter-of-factly. "You see each other

almost every day. Go talk outside. I want to talk about you guys with Stevie."

I blush as they all balk.

"Shoo," Harper commands and they all obey immediately. Bode grabs the plate of burgers and heads outside, sending a wink my way.

"We'll be back." Marcus drops a kiss to her lips and follows the rest of the guys outside.

The low sounds of a cartoon drift into the kitchen with the giggles of the kids. With them entertained, Harper wastes no time bringing up the elephant in the room caused by the news breaking of me and Bode being together.

"Bode says you're having a hard time with things."

I blow out a breath, pulling my sweater tighter around my front. "I swear, hockey players are bigger gossips than my Nan."

Harper lays a warm hand on my forearm. "He only brought it up to Marcus because he's worried about you."

"I don't think I realized how cutting people can be. The number of times I've been called a bitch and a home-wrecker this week? It's exhausting."

"I wish I could tell you it gets easier, but you learn to block out the noise."

"Really? Because it seems like the noise is going to crush me. I never thought it would affect my job. I mean all these canceled appointments? Do they really care that much about my personal life?"

"You've really had that many?" Harper asks.

I nod. "Almost all of my appointments have been canceled. At the rate I'm going, I'll be fired within a week."

"That's strange." She gives me a studious look. "I get Bode is in the limelight, but that's weird."

"I thought so too, but I don't know if I can keep dealing with this."

The number of messages I've gotten over the last week has increased tenfold. When Bode said things would get worse before they get better, I didn't think they'd get this bad. I never knew women could be so bitchy. Bitch and home-wrecker are the nicer of the comments. I haven't told Bode about the bad ones.

What's the point of getting him worked up? I don't want him to spout off in anger and make things worse for himself.

"Look, Stevie. Bode is going to be in the limelight for a long time. He's still in the prime of his career. Can you handle it? I know some wives who get messages from strangers saying they wish they could have a night with their husband and offer ungodly sums of money."

My jaw hits the ground. "Are you serious?"

She nods, sipping her wine. "You don't have to worry about most people. They're respectful and, if they see you out and about, might ask for a selfie and autograph. But there are some that don't have boundaries and have zero shame telling you what they think."

I sip my own wine, letting the warmth of it try to calm my anxious cells. How do I figure out how to deal with Bode's job?

The worst of the attacks have been the ones asking me how Bode could go for anyone like me and wondering how I could tread on another woman's life and steal her man.

Ugly.

Hideous.

A slut.

Only with Bode because of his money and good looks.

It hurts. All I want to do is help make others feel beautiful in their skin. To have these words thrown at me is rocks at glass. I've worked hard to insulate myself from letting harsh words and actions affect me. But when they're coming at me from all directions every minute of the day? I can only do so much to let it roll off my back.

And even worse, I hate burdening Bode with these emotions.

"Listen, I don't want to cause you any more worry, but if you ever need to unload about it, I'm here for you," Harper tells me, bringing me out of my thoughts.

I give her a half-smile. "I appreciate it. Sometimes it feels like I'm out here on an island all by myself."

"Not by yourself. You have me and Bode. And the rest of the guys. Your grandma. We'll help you figure this whole dating a hockey star out."

"Stevie! Look, look!" One of the girls calls out and I'm flying out of my seat, almost knocking my wine over.

"Is everything okay?" I rush into the living room, my heart in my throat.

"Look!"

They point to Caleb. He's standing on his feet in the middle of the living room and takes two hesitant steps before falling.

"Oh my God. Holy shit! Bode. Get in here!"

"What?" He rushes into the kitchen with a spatula in hand, the rest of the guys falling in behind him. "What's wrong? Is it Caleb?"

"Caleb is walking."

"What?" Now Caleb is sitting on the floor between the girls. Jamie is unbothered with the commotion, continuing to watch the show.

Bode thrusts the spatula at Dax and walks into the living room and bends down next to the girls. "Caleb. Are you walking? Can you walk to Daddy?"

Caleb looks like he's deciding before he pushes himself

up. Fishing my phone out of my jeans pocket, I turn the video on, hoping he'll take another step.

"C'mon, Caleb," one of the guys encourages from behind. "You can do it."

"Go, Caleb, go!" the girls cheer in unison.

He's looking around the room at all the people staring at him.

"You can do it," I tell him.

It's not like he can understand me, but I want Bode to see this. With his schedule, there's no telling if he'll be home the next time it happens.

"Show everyone what you just did," Bode tells him. "You can do it."

Then Caleb takes one step and then two more before he starts to fall and Bode scoops him up.

"My kid is amazing!" He holds him up, peppering his face in kisses. "Way to go, buddy!"

"All kids—" Jasper starts, but he can't get a word in edgewise.

"Don't you dare finish that sentence," Harper hisses next to me.

Tears well in my eyes at seeing how happy Bode is. It's the sweetest moment seeing Bode experience this.

Things might be hard right now, but getting to be with Bode during this milestone? Being with Bode?

It's worth all the hard.

Chapter Thirty-One

STEVIE

"Here's your next appointment." Cressy passes over the tablet, giving me the details of my next client.

"I have an appointment?" I question, taking a bite of my apple. I've been sitting in the employee locker room since I got here. Every single one of my appointments for the day have canceled. After canceling yesterday as well.

I got that same sickly-sweet smile from Becky when she told me. It ratcheted up my annoyance having to go back to the locker room and sit for most of my shift.

Again.

It's been crickets for the last week and it has me anxious. I can't keep up like this. I rely on this job to make ends meet.

"You do."

"But I've only had a handful in the last two weeks."

Ever since the media found out who I am, it feels like there has been a target on my back. No one wants me as their aesthetician.

"They didn't fill out the intake form?" Glancing down

at the info, they also booked two back-to-back sessions. "This doesn't make any sense."

"They're waiting for you in your room."

Cressy wiggles her fingers at me and heads back to grab her next client.

What in the world?

Dropping the tablet off at reception, I head to my room and knock on the door. "Hi, I'm—"

I stop dead at the smiling face gazing back at me.

"What in the world are you doing here?" Clicking the door shut softly behind me, I cross my arms and stare at the man sitting on my table.

"I figured I'd see what all you do every day." Bode shrugs a shoulder. "I had time after practice before I need to pick Caleb up from Harper's."

"So you thought you'd come get a facial from me? For two hours?"

Bode holds out a hand to me and I take it, letting him pull me into his legs. The robe he's wearing hints at his strong pecs underneath. Even in a plain robe, he still somehow manages to look sexy.

"Well, I figured I could get a facial and then you and I could—"

I slap a hand over his mouth. "We are not having sex where I work!" I hiss.

"Relax." Bode pulls my hand down. "I want to hang out with you and figured it'd be a nice break for you."

"Oh. That's actually really thoughtful." I press a kiss to his lips. A very chaste, not at all what I want to give him kind of kiss. "Thank you."

"Now, do I get my facial or not?" He waggles his eyebrows at me.

"Yes. But you have to be professional."

"What?" He throws up his hands in defense. "It's not my fault that my aesthetician is the sexiest woman here."

I roll my eyes as I take his robe and hang it on the back of the door. Bode is wearing a pair of black joggers that sit low on his hips. The V leading down into the hint of boxer briefs that are exposed teases me as to what's under them. Hard slabs of muscle are begging to be ogled.

But I can't. Not when I just told him he had to be professional.

"Eyes up here, Stevie," Bode tells me. My gaze snaps to his and a cocky smile torments me.

"Lie down." I try not to laugh, but hold the sheet up for him. Bode gives me a quick peck before he lies down on my table and I cover him up. A shame, really, to hide this gorgeous man. "I'm going to do a skin check before we get started, okay?"

"What's that?"

"I take a look at your face and it gives me an idea of what I'll be doing today. Make sure there are not spots that might be of concern."

"Well then, look away."

He smirks as he shuts his eyes and I cover them with protective eyewear. It's hard to focus when working on his handsome face. Under the harsh lights, I can make out every freckle, every tiny imperfection on his face.

As if there are any.

"How do you wash your face?"

"What do you mean?"

"What do you use? Anything special?"

"A bar of soap when I shower."

"Of course you do." I groan. "You have near perfect skin and basically do nothing to make it that way."

I shut off the light and take off the protective goggles.

"You remember you said that to me one of the first days you moved in?"

"God, don't remind me."

Bode quirks one eye open at me. "It was cute."

"Cute? Really?"

I hit play on the soft, ambient music and smack his shoulder.

"What? You are."

"I don't think I want to be described as cute."

"Well, I have to keep it professional or otherwise I would say all the ways you're not cute."

"Better. Now, eyes closed so *I* can be professional and give you what you're paying way too much for."

Pumping the face wash into my hand, I wet it and start to massage it into Bode's skin. Bode relaxes into the table, letting the cushioned material of the heated table hold him.

I could do this process in my sleep. It's different for each client, based on their needs, but it doesn't vary too much.

"Tell me what you're doing."

"You know,"—I grab another generous amount of cleanser and it squelches between my fingers—"most of my clients don't talk this much."

"You know what I do. I want to know your process."

Grabbing a hot towel, I place it on his neck before covering his face—a shame, really—and gently massaging his face.

"Next I'll do a warm honey cleanser. It'll kill any bacteria on your face. If you're only washing your face at the locker room, you need it."

"Are you going to give me a fancy routine I need to do?"

Pulling the towel off his face, warm brown eyes stare

up at me. "I know better than to tell you what to do. Even if I know better than you, I'll make it easy for you."

Taking the thick, sweet-smelling cream into my hands, I massage it into Bode's face. He sighs as my fingers work their magic.

"It's going to start to feel warm, and I'm going to give it a bit of steam to work its way in."

"This feels incredible. How come I've never done this before?"

"Maybe because you never thought you needed one and only came to rescue me."

"I'd do anything for you, Stevie."

He doesn't open his eyes, so it's easy to let my emotions play out on my face. It's different working on someone you're intimate with. On someone who knows all your dark parts and doesn't flinch in the face of them.

Who is fighting the cruelty I'm continuing to face.

"Let me know if you can feel this." I turn the steamer on and tilt him in that direction.

"Feels good." I massage his shoulders as I let the cleanser work itself into his skin. "Mmm. Doubly good."

"I'm glad."

Kneading his shoulders helps to work out my own tension. I dig my knuckles into the muscles. I know he works hard and I want this to feel good for him.

I work through the rest of my routine, explaining each step to the curious man on my table. By the time I finish up, I feel more calm than I have in weeks.

"Look how good you look." I smile down at him, resting my elbows on the table.

"All thanks to you." Bode grabs my hand and kisses the center of my palm.

"Thank you for coming today."

He gives me a nervous smile. "Still no bookings?"

I shake my head. "No."

"Things will get better. I promise."

Bode sits up and pulls me in close.

"You think so?" I twirl my fingers through the hair at the nape of his neck. His handsome face has a dewy glow. Being in his arms is settling.

"The PR team is working on it, so I'm hoping it'll go back to normal soon."

"It's still out there, Bode."

After my chat with Harper, I deleted my social media altogether. It's not like it's a highlight reel I need to remember. The less chance of coming across a message calling me out, the better.

"You're not alone, okay? Don't carry this by yourself."

A riot of emotions courses through me as I fuse my lips to his. "I love you, Bode."

That earns me a smile. "I know. I love you more, and I'm not going anywhere."

I only hope I can carry this feeling until this thing blows over.

If it blows over.

Chapter Thirty-Two

STEVIE

One appointment.

That's it. After Bode came in yesterday, I have one appointment on the books with a new client. I wonder if they told them who they were scheduling them with.

Even after the Knights issued a statement asking for Bode's privacy, the messages didn't stop. They only increased.

I thought deleting the apps would help, but they somehow got my email. These people are relentless.

Casting stones when they know nothing about me? I hate it.

"Stevie. Can I talk to you after your appointment?" Maryann asks me.

"Sure."

Crap. This can't be good. Having a conversation with your boss when things haven't been going well?

It doesn't make for the most calm environment.

My client is an older woman, which probably explains why when I introduce myself to her, she shows no sign of recognition.

Thank God.

The ritual of my job is the only reason I can get through the next hour. I've done this hundreds of times, so I could do it in my sleep.

If this woman is my only client today, I want to make sure I do my best job.

"How was everything today?" I ask her as she comes out of the room.

"Delightful. I feel ten years younger. Thank you, Miss Stephanie. I'll be sure to ask for you when I come back."

"Thank you."

I show her to the quiet room and write up my notes for her. By the time I'm done, my feet feel like they're walking through cement as I walk to Maryann's office.

I knock on the door and wait for her to call me in.

"You wanted to see me?" I take a seat in front of her desk.

She's the only one of us with an office. Seeing as how she's the manager and spends more of her time away from guests, it makes sense.

"I'm sorry we're having this discussion today, Stevie, as you've always been one of my best aestheticians."

Oh God. My stomach drops and my heart catches in my throat. This isn't good.

"Without your clients, there's been a drop in sales and I'm afraid we're going to have to let you go."

"You're firing me?"

She at least has the decency to look chagrined. "I'm sorry. But we can't keep losing business because of bad press."

"But I haven't done anything wrong."

She leans across her desk. Papers are strewn over it. "Maybe when things settle down, we can talk about you coming back, but for right now, I think this is the best course of action."

Tears well in my eyes. Sure, I've changed jobs over the years because things weren't right, but I've never been fired.

I work hard. I never call in sick and am never late. I don't cause drama.

Because of something out of my control, I'm getting fired for the first time in my twenty-five years.

It feels terrible.

"We'll pay you out two weeks, but today is your last day."

"Right." I stand, my vision blurring in front of me. "I appreciate you giving me this opportunity."

What else can I say? I keep my composure as best I can as I dash to the bathrooms.

Except I'm not the only one in there. Cressy is wiping her hands on a paper towel.

"What's wrong?" she asks, seeing my face.

"I got fired." I burst into tears as Cressy pulls me in for a hug.

"Oh, sweetheart. I'm so sorry."

"It's not like I asked for this to happen. I didn't want people to figure out I'm the one with Bode. And why do people care so much that I'm with him? I didn't think people would be *this* upset."

"They're jealous because they want to be with him and can't be. But it's okay, Stevie. We'll figure this out. I'll help you find another job."

"Who's going to hire me?" I try to stop the tears, but they keep coming. "They'll take one look at me and know who I am."

"Hey." Cressy gives me a squeeze before looking me in

the eye. "We'll figure this out. Not everyone has to follow the Knights."

"In Nashville?" My laugh is watery. "Fat chance of that happening."

"What's Bode said about it?"

I shake my head, wiping my tears away with the sleeve of my work smock. Guess I won't be needing to wear this anymore. "To not let it get to me. That it'll pass in a few weeks and everything will be okay."

"In a few weeks? He can't expect you to be in limbo like that."

"What else can he do? Women keep saying he's the father of their baby. I'm a home-wrecker and a slut and every other crass word out there. He can't wrap me in a bubble."

Cressy looks horrified. "I thought you deleted everything."

"I didn't want you to worry, but they're emailing me now."

"Stephanie Campbell, you are my best friend. Whether you like it or not, I'm going to worry about you. You have to tell me these things."

"You know I hate being a burden."

The look she gives me could melt glass. It has me moving around her and splashing cold water on my face.

"Stevie, babe. You are not a burden. You are never a burden. I don't care how many past boyfriends have told you that having feelings or being vulnerable isn't something they wanted to bear, but it is not true. You have the biggest heart of anyone I know when you let people in. Let people help you and share your worries. I love you, Stevie, and I know Bode does too. Let us be there for you like you're always there for us."

I hold out a hand and she takes it. Hugging her to my side, I rest my head on her shoulder. "Sorry."

"No need to apologize. I'm not going anywhere. I might have to shake you a few times to get you to talk to me about things you keep to yourself, but that's my problem."

I snort a laugh. "Thank you for always being here for me."

"We'll get through this. If I have to raise hell to make sure you get your job back, I will."

"Maybe I can stay at your place for a little while?"

Cressy eyes me with a dubious look. "You have been turning me down left and right, and now you want to stay with me?"

"Only until things die down. Maybe if I'm not around, things will go back to normal. Besides, if they found my email, I don't want them tracking down where I live."

"Oh, Stevie. I am so sorry this is happening."

"Me too."

I thought I was at my lowest before.

It had nothing on this. No job *and* no home?

Guess there are a few more layers I had yet to uncover from rock bottom.

Chapter Thirty-Three

BODE

For once in my life, hockey doesn't bring the escape from my problems that it normally does.

Growing up, whenever I got angry about my lot in life, about my parents not caring or loving me enough, I could take my aggression out on the ice.

A hard workout?

Line drills?

All of it helped calm the raging thoughts in my brain.

When it's happening to someone you love?

There's no stopping the torrent of emotion. She's been withdrawn lately, retreating into herself.

I know the messages she's getting. I only hoped they would stop with the team's statement. It seems she is the scapegoat for everything happening to me.

Even though all the press is fueling my need to play better—I want them to talk about how great I'm playing, and not my personal life—it's not helping.

It's not her fault.

I got myself into this mess before she came along.

Except, Caleb isn't a mess.

Was I expecting a kid to land on my doorstep? No.

But it's the best damn thing to ever happen to me. I wouldn't trade him for the world. I always thought the best thing about me would be being remembered as one of the greatest hockey players for the Knights.

Now, all I want to be is the best dad to Caleb. The best partner to Stevie. They're the most important things in my life.

"You doing okay?" Dax asks me. "You've been distracted all day."

"Sorry. This shit with Stevie is messing with my head."

"How's she doing with all of it?" He wipes a towel over his face. The locker room is sweltering after practice.

"Honestly? She's not handling it well."

"I'm sorry. That really sucks, man. I wish I could help."

I clap him on the shoulder. "I appreciate you guys being here for me. That's about all you can do."

"We've got your back. If you want us to find them and take them out, we can."

"We can?" Jasper questions, walking up to us. "I don't think I signed up for that."

Dax rolls his eyes. "I volunteered you. If you needed to take someone out, we'd do it for you."

"If I ever find myself in that situation, I sure as shit am not asking you first. You guys are the least subtle people around."

"As fun as this is," I say to end this conversation before they really get rolling, "I need to get home. I'll see you guys later."

"Remember, we can take them out!" Dax calls out behind me.

I wave behind me and head straight to my truck. By the time I make it home, Stevie's car is already in the drive-way. Not in the garage where she usually parks.

Why does that cause dread to wash over me?

The fact that she's home in the middle of the day is also worrisome. I was hoping to have a few hours to figure out what I could say or do to make this whole situation better.

"Stevie?" Heading inside, I call out for her. I drop my hockey bag in the laundry room as I walk down the hall.

Two bags are sitting by the front door.

Crap.

"Stevie? Where are you?"

"I'm in here."

I follow the sound of her voice into the living room. She looks absolutely gutted, sitting there stiff as a board.

"What's wrong?" I hurry around to her, dropping to my knees.

Red-rimmed eyes greet me. I hate seeing how sad she looks. Those blue eyes should never hold an ounce of pain.

"I got fired."

"What? How? They can't do that."

I brush the fresh tears rolling down her cheeks with my thumb.

"I was costing them too much business. They couldn't afford to keep me on."

"Because…because of everything that's been happening?"

She nods.

"Fuck. Stevie, I am so sorry. Can I call and try and talk to your boss? Figure something out?"

She shakes her head, tucking a loose blonde hair behind her ear. "It hasn't stopped, Bode. They got my email and I can't take it anymore."

"What does that mean?" I swallow the emotion choking my throat. It's hard to breathe as she stands and starts pacing the living room.

"What if they find out I'm staying here, Bode? What if it escalates? I can't stomach the idea of something happening to you or Caleb or our grandmas."

"You realize the two of them are a home security system in themselves, right? They'd take anyone out." I try to add levity to the situation, but it's no use.

I've never seen Stevie like this.

"But it could happen. Until this thing blows over, I'm going to go and stay with Crestina for a while."

"Please don't."

"I'll be back when this blows over."

I stand and take her into my arms. I try to memorize every curve and dip. Because right now, it feels like she's leaving.

For good.

"It doesn't feel like that. Please don't go," I beg.

"I can't be here right now, Bode. It hurts too much."

"Stevie. It'll blow over."

It feels like a lie coming from my lips. But what else can I say to get her to stay?

"As long as I'm around, they're going to keep coming after you."

"But…" I don't even know what to say.

Don't go?

Stay?

I love you?

The bags by the front door tell me Stevie's mind is made up.

"I love you, Bode. But I just need to clear my head. Try to find stable footing."

She turns on her heel without looking at me. Desperation claws at my insides. I can't lose her. "Stevie. Please."

It's a plea, nothing short of me begging on my knees for her to stay.

"I'll be back."

"Promise?" My voice is soft, emotion strangling me.

She smiles, but says nothing else as she grabs her things and heads out the front door. The sound of her engine rumbles through the house before it disappears altogether.

"Fuck!" I shout. "Fuck!"

I hate this. My heart feels like it's cracking in my chest.

It doesn't feel like Stevie is going to be back. It feels like she ripped my heart out and took it with her.

I hate that my playboy past is causing a divide between the two of us. We all have a past and I thought I was finally moving beyond mine. That I could have a future with this woman. A family.

I wanted my private life to stay private.

Turns out, it's out there for the entire world to see now.

Chapter Thirty-Four

BODE

MARCUS

Want to go out tonight? Harper is taking the
girls to a movie

BODE

Gran is going out with Deb

Just me and the little guy

JASPER

You need a night out

Nah, I'm good

Not in the mood anyway

DAX

Sitting at home and stewing isn't good

Who said I'm stewing?

NOAH

I can tell you're stewing from here

GRAHAM

He would know

GRAHAM

He's an excellent stewer

NOAH

Am not!

MARCUS

What they mean to say is why don't we come over and we can hang out?

I promise, I'm fine

JASPER

Fine, be that way

I'm not being any way

MARCUS

We'll deal with you tomorrow at practice

Nothing to deal with

I'm fine

MARCUS

When Harper says that, it's the exact opposite

Then I'm terrible

JASPER

Now that we believe

What's that, Caleb? You're hungry?

Gotta go

MARCUS

You're an ass

Love you too

"Are you going to be okay on your own tonight?" Gran asks me.

Caleb is stumbling around on the floor, learning his way. Ever since he took his first steps, I found every single baby-proofing item I didn't have so I could protect him. When I debated getting a helmet for him, Gran threatened to make me wear my own helmet around.

I backed off immediately.

"We'll be fine."

"You sure?" Caleb waddles over to her and she scoops him up, peppering him with kisses.

I sigh, sinking into the couch and wanting it to swallow me whole. "Yes. We'll be good. I've got this whole dad thing down now."

That earns me a smile from the baby in her arms. I'm choosing to believe he can understand me and likes me being his dad.

Gran pats my cheek. "I never thought I'd see the day when you'd be okay with him on your own."

I smile down at my son's happy face. "Yeah, we're good."

I never thought I'd want to stay in on a Friday night. But honestly? There's not many people I want to see right now.

"I'm proud of you, you know that, right?" Gran asks me, walking around the couch and dropping onto the end of the chaise. "Not many people would have stepped up like you did."

"I honestly didn't think I had it in me," I confess. "I worry I'm going to fail Caleb every day."

Gran laughs and that has my attention swinging to hers.

"Oh, honey. Welcome to parenthood. That will never go away. Just wait until he becomes a teenager."

"Fuck." I scrub a hand down my face. The tiny bundle in my arms giggles. "You're looking forward to that, aren't you?"

"It's even harder doing it alone, but you're not."

I nod my head. "I know."

"We're all here for you. Whatever you need, my sweet boy."

"Thanks, Gran. I love you."

"I know. I love you too." She drops a kiss onto the top of my head. "Deb and I are heading out. Don't wait up for us."

"Don't do anything I wouldn't do," I yell after her.

She waves her hand in acknowledgment and is out the front door. The minute it closes behind her, it's quiet.

Too quiet.

Except for the sound of Caleb blabbering. Until he very clearly says, "Dada."

"Oh my God. Can you say that again? Dada. That's me."

"Dadadada."

I sweep him up into the air, loving the sound of those words coming from him. "Stevie—"

Fuck. She's not here. I can't share in the excitement of this moment with her.

She's been gone for two weeks and I hate it. I hate how silent the house is without her. I hate not seeing her every morning. Having her smile welcome me home. Playing games with her. Laughing with her.

Fuck. I miss everything about her.

I thought things would settle down once the team issued a statement, but they haven't. And I'm pissed.

Pissed off to the point where I'm having someone dig into how they got Stevie's email.

Just thinking about how much pain they've caused her

makes my own heart ache. Ache at how much I miss her. Miss just spending a night in with her. I never thought I was the settling down type. That I would grow old with one person and want that more than anything else in life.

My life has two eras—before Caleb and Stevie, and after. Looking back, I really don't like the person that I was. Everything I did was to not feel. Turns out, that was not the way to go through life. Sitting with my thoughts on my own? I hated it.

Stevie made me confront all of that. Made it easier to come to terms with.

Her confidence made me believe in myself. Made me believe I could actually be a good dad to Caleb.

There isn't one trace of who I was before him in this house. The TV? Playing a kids' show that I find I don't hate. Toys of all kinds are spread out on Caleb's play mat. Baby blankets and wash cloths sit in a neat pile at the end of the couch. Something to put away once he goes to bed. The wet bar? Yeah, all that alcohol has sat untouched for months. It's now stocked with all of Caleb's food.

"Would you be okay if it was just the two of us?"

Caleb stares up at me like I'm the best thing in the world. He's the best thing in mine. I would do anything for him. Hell, if I had to retire tomorrow, I would.

Not that he would ask that of me considering he can only say *Dada*, but still.

I'd do it.

A knock sounds at the door. Glancing up, the porch light is shining on a group of familiar guys. I stand up and walk over to let them in.

"What are you guys doing here?"

Dax, Graham, and Noah all brush by me and head inside. Dax holds up a six-pack of my favorite beer. "We figured you'd be a bit down after everything that happened."

"Jasper had plans," Graham tells me. "And everyone in Marcus's house is sick, so he stayed home to take care of them."

I smile at that. "Probably a good thing. I don't want to get Caleb sick."

Noah cracks open a beer and hands one over to me. "Exactly what we said."

"Thanks." I take a long pull before setting it down and shifting Caleb in my arms. "I appreciate you guys coming over."

"I can safely say having a broken heart is the worst," Noah tells me.

"Can't say I like it," I confirm.

"Is this really the first time you've ever had your heart broken?" Dax asks.

I nod. "When you never settle down, it's hard for it to happen."

"Damn."

And this is exactly why. That knife in my heart? I never want to experience this feeling again.

"Are you just going to sit back and let it happen?" Graham asks.

"What can I do? It's not like she signed up for this life."

Hell, it's the least favorite part of the job. Having a camera shoved in my face after every game? Having women come out of the woodwork to say I fathered their kid?

Yeah, it fucking sucks.

"I don't believe that it's over for a second," Noah tells me, settling into one of the barstools. "What are you going to do about it?"

"What do you mean?" I set Caleb in his green foam

seat by me and cross my arms. "She doesn't want any part of this life."

Graham waves me off. "Noah's right. This life is hard. I don't know if I could do it with someone who didn't understand what we go through."

"Why would anyone choose this lifestyle?" I say more to myself than anything.

My past coming to meet my future? I don't know if it will ever stop. It hasn't since Stevie left. I'm really good at ignoring the noise, but why would she want to?

"What it boils down to is if you love her," Dax tells me.

I study him. "When did you get so smart?"

He lets out a long-suffering sigh. "My brother is getting married."

Noah chokes on his beer and Graham nearly spits his out. "Are you shitting me? Who would be dumb enough to marry him?"

I know Noah's sister used to date Duncan until she caught him cheating on her. He got bounced from the Black Diamonds because of sleeping with an assistant coach's wife from what I heard.

"Chloe."

"Wait, why does that name sound familiar?" Noah asks.

"Because it's Dax's best friend," Graham finishes.

"Oh, shit. Are you serious?" I ask.

Dax slams the rest of his beer and nods his head. "I don't know how it happened, but it did."

"Wow. I'm sorry."

He winces. "Yeah. It sucks."

"Anything we can do to help?" I ask.

Dax smiles over at me. "Yeah, you can fix things with Stevie to distract me from my brother's upcoming nuptials."

"How do I even know if she'll want me back? I can't keep chasing someone that doesn't want me. It's not fair to either of us. Or Caleb."

Caleb chooses that moment to start screaming, "Dada."

"Did he really just say that?" Noah asks. "Do you know who Dada is?"

Caleb looks at me like the person talking to him is crazy.

"That's so cute he said that." Noah turns to Graham. "Maybe we need one of these."

I grab Caleb. He looks so proud of himself. His hair is a mess, but he's wearing the giraffe outfit Stevie got him.

"Find your own kid."

"Damn," Graham says. "And here I thought we could just take him home."

Noah laughs, taking a drink of his beer. "Well, we'll be here for him if he ever needs anything. The cool uncles."

My heart blooms. I have more people who love me in my life than I ever thought possible. It doesn't matter that I had a shitty childhood or parents that ran out.

I had Gran. I didn't make things easy for her, but she still loved me.

Caleb's mom is out of the picture. She terminated her rights with a note to not contact her. Considering I was in a trance those first few weeks, trying to figure out her motivations was the furthest thing from my mind.

It was okay though, because we had Stevie.

"Please," Dax scoffs. "I'm going to be Caleb's favorite uncle."

"We'll give you that. Each of us can be a favorite," Noah tells him.

I smile at that. "Just like you're Sam and Sadie's favorite uncles?"

"Hey." He points a finger in my face. "I am the favorite uncle."

"Keep dreaming," Graham jests.

"At least I get to be Caleb's," Dax says.

"What if Jasper is his favorite?" Noah goads him.

Dax rolls his eyes. "Please. Jasper would probably scare him."

"He's not here to defend himself," I tell them. "At least try to pretend he's in the running."

"Nah." Dax wiggles his fingers in front of Caleb. "I'm claiming the title of favorite uncle. You can't take it back."

"That's it."

"What's it?" they all ask.

It hits me like a lightning bolt. What I need to do to get Stevie back once and for all.

That one move of his hand.

The hand flex.

What Stevie loves.

I don't want Stevie to be the one that got away. She's too important. I love her too much.

I have to show her how much she means to me. That we can weather any storm *together*. That she doesn't have to run when things get hard.

I need to channel my inner Darcy and let her know just how much she means to me. And that I'll never let her get away.

Chapter Thirty-Five

STEVIE

No. No. No. Definitely not, no.

Not having a job is the worst. I've been doing nothing but looking for available jobs and applying until my fingers hurt. I don't want to be picky, but I don't think my car could make an hour round-trip drive every day.

It's been crickets. All of the hiring immediately ads are lying. I have experience. If you don't actually want someone, then why say that?

Ugh. I hate how angry I'm feeling right now. It's not helping anything. My phone buzzes on the nightstand next to me.

My heart drops at the name on my phone. Every time it rings, I'm secretly hoping it's Bode.

He's giving me my space like I asked for.

"Hey Harper."

"Good, you answered," she tells me by way of greeting.

"Why wouldn't I answer?" I lie back against the oversized pillows. Thankfully Cressy's guestroom was ready for me. It might not have much besides a bed, nightstand, and dresser, but it's all I need.

"I was worried you'd be upset with me."

"Why would I be upset with you?"

"Because of everything that's happened."

I wince, rubbing a hand over my forehead. I'm going to get wrinkles early from all the tension headaches I've had. "It's not your fault."

"I know, but I feel terrible. I wish I could do more."

"You're still here."

"How are things?" she asks.

"Well, the emails have slowly started to taper off."

"If I were you, I'd change my email," she tells me.

I laugh. "You are not the first person to tell me that. But is it weird I want to keep it? To see when this all goes away?"

Because then, maybe I can be back in Bode's arms. I can't do it if they're still at risk.

I won't endanger them.

"As long as you're deleting them immediately and not opening them."

"I'm not, I promise. But hopefully they will stop soon. I don't know why."

"I—"

"Holy shit. Look at this!" Cressy comes busting in my room.

"Oh my god. Knock much?"

Even though the door was mostly open, the bang startles me.

"Is everything okay?" Harper asks.

"No, it's not," Cressy tells her. "Look."

She shoves her phone in my face. Leaning back so I can look at it, my jaw drops.

"Holy shit."

"What? What is it? I can't see!" Harper's voice rings out over the phone.

"It's an email. From Becky."

"Who's that?" she asks.

"Did she really send this?" I ask, looking back at Cressy. "I can't believe it was her."

It's another email blasting me for being a homewrecker and a terrible person. It seems the copy and paste didn't work right, because there's also a comment at the end about canceling someone's appointment.

"Oh, you bet your ass it was. She loves the Knights. She was jealous."

"But…I hardly ever work with her. She acts like she's better than me most of the time."

I can't believe she would do this.

"Not anymore."

Cressy taps away on the phone as I explain what's going on to Harper. I peer over my best friend's shoulder to see what she's typing.

CRESTINA

Have you really been sending these?
<<screenshot of email>>

BECKY

What? That wasn't me

CRESTINA

Then why is it your email?

BECKY

I was hacked

CRESTINA

Nice try

CRESTINA

I'll be reporting you to Maryann first thing tomorrow

BECKY

It wasn't me!

CRESTINA

Please. Of course it was

CRESTINA

I can't believe you would do this

BECKY

Why should she get the man and not me?

"OKAY, I'm half tempted to come over right now and see what is going on."

I shake my head, even though she can't see it. "We'll get drinks next week. I need to figure out what's going on myself."

"Okay. Keep me updated, okay?" Harper tells me.

"I will."

"Oh! And before I forget," Harper starts, "I have a line on a new job for you."

"Really? Where?"

"I'll text it to you, okay? It's where my massage therapist works."

"That'd be amazing. Thanks, Harper. Really."

"I've got your back, Stevie. I'll see you next week."

Ending the call, I toss the phone onto the bed and grab Cressy's phone.

"I can't believe she would stoop so low," she says.

"I never thought someone I work with would do this. I feel…"

Heartbroken. Betrayed. Angry.

"Too many things. Take some time to process, and maybe it means things will finally end."

"You think so?"

She nods. "Yes. And you bet your ass I'm telling Maryann. I can't believe she would jeopardize her own job like that."

"Probably didn't think she'd get caught," I mutter.

"Ladies, dinner will be here in a few," Dylan calls out.

Cressy runs out, giving me time to try and come to terms with what all is happening. I can't believe it was Becky.

Now that we know who did this, I'm guessing it'll stop. Maybe I could get my job back. But do I want to work somewhere that dropped me without questioning anything?

That's a problem for tomorrow. Right now, I'm ravenous and need something to eat.

Grabbing a sweatshirt, I pull it on over my head and walk into the living room.

"Uhh, you're not the delivery guy," Cressy tells whoever is in the hallway.

She swings the door open and there's Bode. He's a feast for my sore and tired eyes. He doesn't look like he's faring much better than I am.

I drink him in. The way his hair is a mess. The exhaustion clinging to his face. What I'm only assuming is part of Caleb's dinner splattered on the pocket of his hoodie.

"What are you doing here?"

"I need to talk to you."

My eyes dart to Cressy. She's looking between the two of us, and Dylan is ignoring us entirely.

"Why don't the two of us get out of your hair?" Cressy walks over to the couch and shuts off the TV.

That gets Dylan's attention. "Hey. I was playing that."

"We need to go."

"Didn't we order dinner?" he asks.

"We'll grab it downstairs and have a picnic. Get moving," Cressy barks.

"Wow." Dylan only now realizes who is in his living room. "Uhh, do you know who you are?"

"Not now, Dylan," Cressy says, hurrying him out the door. She shoots me a wink and closes the door behind her.

"What are you doing here?"

Bode stalks toward me, hoisting me into his arms and taking me into my room. "Taking you home."

He sets me on the edge of the dresser. "What?"

"Here. Look."

Bode pulls out his phone and shows me the screen. It's a picture of the Knights social media account.

The Nashville Knights have issued a statement on behalf of their star forward, Bode Adams, who has been in the press for his new relationship with Stephanie Campbell, and the appearance of his son.

"I want to thank the Knights for their continued support of me and my personal life. Being in the limelight is not easy, but it is something I chose. I love this sport and this team and wouldn't change any of it.

The people in my life did not ask for this. They did not ask to have their personal information on the internet for all to see. The invasion of privacy is abhorrent. The bullying and invasive comments must stop. I cannot be at my best when I am worrying about those I love.

For those that have continued dragging my name and the names of those I love through the mud, I humbly ask that you stop. For the good of my child, those I love, and everyone close to me.

For the fans that have done nothing but support me, thank you. Thank you for welcoming me to Nashville and letting me be a part of this team. I love it, and hope to play my entire career here."

"YOU DID THIS?" My jaw is on the ground. "But why?"

"Why?" Bode shakes his head. "Because I love you, Stevie. I would do anything to protect you and I'm sorry I waited so long to do it. I thought the statement from the team would be enough, but it wasn't."

"Well, between this and figuring out who was behind the emails, I have a feeling it might end."

"Wait, what?" He looks confused.

I nod. "Becky, from work. She was sending the emails. She accidentally sent one to Cressy and left part of a cancellation at the bottom."

"Holy shit. I can't believe that. I've never met the woman before."

"And yet, she felt she was entitled to you. She probably sent my name to the press."

"Well, if she did, we'll know. I had someone looking into it. Good thing she copied the wrong person."

"I really hope it's over. I hate people thinking I'm a terrible person," I confess.

"If it helps," he starts, "people are now supporting me, having my back. They can't believe others would behave that way."

"Between this and figuring out it was Becky, I think the emails and messages will stop. I shouldn't have kept checking, but I was hoping the nastiness would go away."

"I think it will." There's a fierceness to his words that makes me believe him.

"I'm sorry this ever happened."

Tears gather in my eyes. It feels like they've been a permanent fixture there. "But it's over. I really think it is."

"Me too."

"Oh, Bode." This time, I can't help crying. Everything I've been feeling the last few weeks comes out.

The anger. The frustration. The sadness.

I let it all go. Safe in Bode's arms.

"I love you, Stevie."

He repeats it over and over, sinking his fingers into my hair and holding me close. By the time the tears subside, Bode is wiping them away. A tender look sits on his handsome face.

"What?"

He smiles, so big it threatens to overwhelm me in the best way. "You have bewitched me, body and soul."

My heart splits wide open for this man who loves me so much, he is quoting my favorite movie to me. "Do you realize how much I love *you* right now?"

"Most ardently, I hope."

I kiss him, smothering his face in kisses. "Darcy doesn't hold a candle to you."

"I will spend our entire lives making sure you know just how much I love you, Stevie. Protecting you from people that want to hurt you and tear you down. And look, if you're not ready to move in with me, I have all your rent money for you to help you find a good place. Even if you want to stay here, I'll still come over and see you as often as I can."

"You still have my rent money?" I ask. Of course he didn't do anything with it. "Why am I not surprised?"

"It's yours. We'll go find a place this weekend."

I shake my head. "We're not doing that."

"No?" He quirks a brow at me.

I push the floppy hair off his forehead, taking him in,

letting him see how serious I am. I never expected to find him, but I love Bode more than I ever thought possible. "Take me home, Bode. Where I belong."

"Damn right." He beams. "You belong with us."

For the first time in my life, it's the truth. It's where I belong. With Bode. I've never felt so loved or so safe as I do with him.

He's my safe place. A place I never want to leave.

As long as I have Bode, I'll have everything I need.

Chapter Thirty-Six

BODE

"Could you not drive any faster?" Stevie whines from next to me.

"I'm trying not to break the law here. I don't need a mugshot plastered all over the news."

Not when things have finally changed for good.

"Well, hurry up. It's been too long and all I want to do is be with you."

"Fuck. We really should have done this at Cressy's."

"And have them interrupt us? No, thanks."

After what feels like hours, my house finally comes into view.

"Finally." Stevie unclicks her seatbelt and climbs over the console. "I've missed you so much."

"You know, you didn't have to leave."

"I was scared they'd find you.'

I brush the soft locks out of her face. "Let me worry about that if it happens again."

"Okay." Her smile is soft and happy. "Now, take me inside."

Lifting Stevie out of the car, I lick and suck on her

neck, reveling in the taste and feel of her as I carry her inside. Even a few weeks was too long without her.

"I never want to be without you again."

Pushing her against the wall, I take my time. I know Caleb is in good hands with Gran.

"Did you hear that?" I hear someone ask.

But before I can take her upstairs, a bucket of ice water is dumped over me.

"What are you doing back?"

Pulling my mouth away from Stevie, I see Gran and Deb are on the couch, blanket covering themselves.

"Oh my God!" I jump back, hitting my back against the wall before turning away entirely. Stevie's holding on to me like a spider monkey. "What are you two doing?"

"Us? The two of you were practically humping in the hallway," Gran counters.

"You said you were going to be a few hours," Deb adds.

My hand is covering my eyes. At this point, I think I need bleach to unsee what I just saw.

Gran and Deb? Really?

"Are you decent?" I hear Stevie ask.

"We're decent," Deb says.

"Are you sure?" I plead.

"They are." Stevie's warm hand rests on my forearm and pulls it away from my eyes. The two women are sitting on the couch with matching smiles.

"Is this funny?"

They look at each other and shrug. "I mean, kind of."

"How long has this been going on?" I wave a finger between the two. "And follow up, where is Caleb?"

"Sleeping upstairs."

"Is this what you two do when we're not home?"

Gran rolls her eyes at me. "You make us sound like

horny teenagers. We watch movies, take Caleb for walks. Eat together."

"Besides, we only go to the movies and make out when you're home."

She says it so casually, as if stating a fact like the sky is blue.

"To the movies. To make out," I groan. "I really didn't need to know that."

"Oh relax," Gran tells me. "We're adults. We're allowed to do what we want."

"Did you know about this?" I turn to Stevie.

"I didn't. I promise. But—"

"But what?"

The look of love is on her face. "I mean, if they're happy, what does it matter?"

"Oooh, someone is all loved up," Deb croons. "I take it by the mutual hump—"

"Please don't finish that sentence. I beg you."

"Oh, like it's any better seeing your grandson and his girlfriend macking on each other?" Gran asks.

"Macking? Really?"

Jesus. I need a drink.

Stalking to the fridge, I open it and pull out one of the first things I find. I need it if we're going to keep having this conversation.

"I think it's sweet," Stevie tells them.

"See?" Deb agrees. "Besides, you two wouldn't have met if I didn't come with Eve."

"Wait." I hop up on the counter. I figure this is as safe a place as any. I'd get my ass handed to me by Gran if I went upstairs to hide out with Caleb. "Is that why Deb came with you?"

Gran rolls her eyes. "You sweet, oblivious boy. Why would I bring a friend to live with me?"

"I don't know. So you don't get lonely?"

"I have a good life. And while I might occasionally get lonely, it's nice to have a companion."

My eyes flit to Stevie. That, I can understand.

"How did this happen?" I ask. "Oh God, and please don't give me the birds and the bees talk. I know that. I mean, how did you two start?"

Stevie giggles at my horror and comes over to stand between my legs.

The two share a tender look. It's obvious they care for one another. If I'm being honest with myself, I don't think I've ever seen Gran look happier.

"We met at bridge, and bridge turned into other card games, which turned into gossiping about the old hags that cheat."

"Oh, not this again," Bode says. "Not everyone is cheating."

"They are too!" Deb says. "No one is that good at bridge."

"Some people are," Stevie whispers.

"Probably where you get it," I lean down, my words ghosting the shell of her year.

"Anyway," Deb continues, "it just sort of happened one night. We fell in love and that was that."

"You're dating then?" I ask.

"If you want to call it that. Do people really date at our age? We're enjoying each other's company."

"You two are 'enjoying each other's company.' Stevie and I are dating." I drop my chin onto Stevie's shoulder. "Why does this feel shockingly normal?"

She spins, looking up at me with nothing but love in her eyes. "Because nothing about our lives is normal. Our grandmas are in love. Who cares?"

"See? Stevie has the right idea," Gran says.

"Shh. I think Bode is finally on board. Don't scare him off," Deb whispers. Or in her impression of a whisper.

"There's a new rule," I tell them, glaring back and forth. "Since it seems like we're all coupled up, no more making out or doing other things on the couch."

Gran studies me with a quizzical stare. "If we can't, that means you can't either."

"It's my house. I should get to do what I want."

"You think I want to come walking in here and see your bare ass? No, thank you." Gran laughs.

I can't help but laugh with her. Because that's the last thing I would want to have happen to me.

"And Caleb can't be in the room, either. No shocking his poor little eyes."

"That was already a given." Gran waves me off and grabs Deb's hand. "Now that this is all settled, why don't you order some dinner for us and we'll all reconvene in the kitchen when it's here?"

I can't even agree before they're closing the back door and hurrying out to the pool house.

"I cannot believe we walked in on that."

Sliding off the counter, I bypass the couch and go straight upstairs. Whatever I was feeling earlier is gone. But that doesn't mean I don't want a quiet moment with Stevie.

Anywhere but the couch right now.

"I mean, I'm glad they found each other. Otherwise, we wouldn't have found one another," Stevie says.

Closing my bedroom door, I guide Stevie toward the bed.

I press a warm kiss to her lips before sitting next to her and pulling her back with me. "Thank God for bridge then."

"Maybe we can have a double date and they can teach us how to play."

I tickle her side. "What, so you can be better at it than I am?"

"Stop it!" she laughs. "I can't help if I get Nan's natural talent at winning games."

"Luck. It's all luck, *Stephanie*."

She throws one leg over me and rests her elbows on either side of my head. "I guess it was a stroke of luck the two of us met."

"I guess it was." I tuck her hair behind her ear. "I'll take that luck."

Stevie looks down at me with nothing but love.

I'm not the hockey player with a history to her. I'm just Bode. Our future is whatever we want to make it. With Caleb and two crazy grandmothers.

It's more than I ever could have asked for.

Epilogue

"You know, I'm happy we have a night out together, but is it weird I miss Caleb?"

Bode stuffs his phone in his suit pants pocket as he helps me out of the car. "No. Because I just got ripped a new one from Gran for checking on him. Again."

I smile, linking my hand with Bode's. "Well, we are going to have some drinks tonight. Dance."

Bode pulls me in front of him, burying his face in my neck. "Maybe make out a bit on the way home."

Heat gathers in my core at the thought of it.

"Mmm. Yes, please."

"Hopefully it's a fast wedding."

I laugh at that. "I don't think any wedding is fast."

"Damn. And here I was hoping we could sneak away for a bit."

"Well, I'm not saying we can't do that. But maybe let's wait until after dinner."

"Right."

Walking with him down the sidewalk toward the park

where Dax's brother is getting married, I see the guys and Harper standing around a high-top table.

"Finally. What took you guys so long?" Harper says by way of greeting. "Just leaving me here with the guys."

"Sorry." I greet her with a side hug and a peck on the cheek. "Caleb was fussy about dinner."

Harper reaches behind her and grabs a glass of champagne to hand over. "Well, you're here now and you look gorgeous."

"Thank you." I take a swig of the bubbly drink before looking down at my dress once again. When Bode told me the dress code, I opted to buy something new.

A formal wedding called for a floor-length navy dress with a thigh-high slit and a sweetheart neckline.

If Bode had convinced me to go back upstairs after he saw me in this dress, we would have been even later.

"You look amazing too." I finger the sparkly gold material of her sequined dress. "Stunning."

"I'm glad you're here." Harper leans close, whispering to me. "I'm still not sure why we're here when we don't even know Duncan."

"Not as quiet as you think, Harper," Marcus says, tugging her back to his side.

"Well, excuse me. I've never met Duncan before in my life."

"We're here for Dax," Jasper points out.

"Double bonus we get a night out." I nudge Harper in the side.

The man we're all here supporting jogs up to our group.

"Hey man," Bode greets him, bringing him in for a clap on the back. "You did a great job organizing everything."

"I mean, yeah." He scrubs a nervous hand down the back of his neck. "It's what Chloe wanted."

Chairs are spread out in front of a pergola, wrapped in vines of flowers. A trail of candles lines the aisle.

A live band is set up, playing a sweet tune. With the reception area behind the ceremony, a wooden dance floor is already set up with the tables and chairs, complete with welcome drinks.

"Are you okay?" I ask, because Dax seems a bit stressed. "I thought you'd be happy that your brother was marrying your best friend."

"Right. Excuse me."

Dax leaves, a sad look washing over his face.

"Is he okay?" Harper asks.

"Looks fine to me." Jasper shrugs.

Harper rolls her eyes. "Of course you would think so."

"It's because Dax is in love with Chloe," Bode clarifies.

"Then why is he here?" Jasper asks.

"Because Chloe is his best friend." Noah's *duh* is implied. "And he wants to support her."

"At least someone gets it," Harper says.

"Hey, I got it," Bode says.

"I got it, but I didn't need to say it," Marcus points out. "I live with three women. I know these things."

"Good job." Harper pecks his cheek.

"I know we were running late, but shouldn't this be starting soon?" Bode asks, glancing at his watch.

"It should be," Graham says. "I'm ready for the reception."

"Me too," I whisper to Bode, sliding a hand around his waist.

The way he looks at me sends butterflies swarming in my belly. God, I love this man. Ever since Bode told me about the big day, I've been daydreaming about our wedding.

What it would look like. Who would be invited. Where it would be.

Honestly?

I don't care about any of that as long as the man standing next to me is there.

It's all I need in life.

Bode and Caleb.

"Okay, it really should have started by now," Marcus points out.

Chatter grows louder as people start looking around. We're not the only people to have noticed this.

"Well, I don't know what's going on, but something's up."

Bode holds out his phone, showing a text from Dax to the guys.

DAX

Enjoy the reception. Gotta go

"GOTTA GO? WHO SAYS THAT?" Jasper asks, shaking his head.

Before anyone can say anything else, the guys are all typing away on their screens.

BODE

Gotta go?

BODE

Dax, it's a wedding

> BODE
>
> What's come up?

MARCUS

Chloe is your best friend

MARCUS

Doesn't matter that it's your brother

NOAH

I still object

NOAH

Duncan's a dick

GRAHAM

We know that

JASPER

But what's come up?

DAX

Umm...

> BODE
>
> This doesn't sound good

MARCUS

What did you do?

DAX

It wasn't me!

DAX

Swear to god

JASPER

What's going on?

DAX

You'll find out soon enough

MARCUS

As your captain, I order you to tell me

BODE

Does that actually work on anyone?

MARCUS

Yes

JASPER

Not me

MARCUS

Didn't say it was you

MARCUS

But I'm using it now

BODE

Tell us, Dax

NOAH

Yeah, c'mon

GRAHAM

Is everything okay?

BODE

Now you're worrying us

DAX

Wedding's off

DAX

Chloe needs a ride

BODE

WTF?

MARCUS

Seriously?

JASPER

What's going on?

JASPER

Why's it off?

NOAH

Because Duncan is a dick

GRAHAM

No other reason needed

MARCUS

No, I'm going to need to know what's going on

MARCUS

Our little Dax doesn't do things like this

BODE

Dax

BODE

Where'd you go?

BODE

Hello?

"OH SHIT," Bode mutters.

"Is this really happening?" Marcus asks.

"This is not like Dax," Jasper says.

"Can you please fill the two of us in on what's going on?" Harper asks, waving her hands between the two of us.

"The wedding is apparently off, and Chloe just left with Dax."

"What the fuck is going on?" a voice I don't recognize shouts behind me.

Startling, I turn, seeing someone that looks remarkably like Dax.

Oh shit.

"I repeat…what the *fuck* is going on?"

"Duncan. How's it going?" Noah asks, a knowing grin on his face.

"How's it going? How's it *going*?" I don't think I've ever seen someone so mad before. "Well, my bride just left, so it's fucking terrible, Noah."

"She left?" Noah asks. He probably shouldn't be grinning as widely as he is, but considering Bode told me that he cheated on Noah's sister, I can't blame him. "Sorry, man. That sucks."

"Fuck you, Fields."

Duncan stalks off, leaving all of us to ourselves.

"So…does this mean we aren't getting dinner?" Graham asks.

Bonus Scene

"Is he finally asleep?" Bode asks.

He's stretched out on the bed, the low glow of the nightstand light illuminating him. His chest is bare and oh so delicious.

"Yes. He's finally asleep." Caleb is in his terrible twos—not wanting to go to sleep. Tonight though, was an easy night. After running around with him at the zoo all afternoon, he was out like a light.

Setting the monitor on the dresser, I cross the space to join my man in bed.

Bode pulls the bedspread back and I snuggle into his side.

"You know, this is one of the last few nights together that we're going to get before the playoffs," he tells me.

"Well, I really hope there's a lot of road trips."

He smirks at me, cupping my cheek. "Are you already trying to get rid of me?"

I nip at his bottom lip. "No. Because I want you to bring you-know-what home."

I want it as badly as he does. I was told I'm not allowed

to say the name of it because we don't want to jinx it. With Bode's schedule being packed these next few weeks, our grandmas are on a trip. It's going to be the three of us holding down the fort.

The Knights played better than I've ever seen them this season. Bode? Well, he's the star of the team, in my humble opinion. I couldn't be more proud of him and the team.

"You know, it's also one of the last few nights that we'll be alone."

"Oh yeah?"

Sliding my hand down his bare chest, he's wearing nothing. A sly grin spreads across his face when my hand closes around his already hard cock.

"Care to make it memorable?" He asks. His brown eyes star down at me.

"Every night with you is memorable." I squeeze his cock, feeling it hardening in my hand. "But let's make this one count, shall we?"

"You don't have to tell me twice, baby."

His mouth captures mine and lust spreads through. Every time I'm with Bode feels like the first time.

Anticipation.

Desire.

Need.

It all spreads through me as his tongue slides against mine. My pussy grows wet as he deepens the kiss.

Hot. Hard. Hungry. Bode devours my mouth as his fingers dig into my side. My hips arch off the bed as he grinds down on me.

I tear my lips from his. "Bode. Take off my clothes."

"Not yet." He trails warm, wet kisses down my neck. Strong fingers toy with the hem of the t-shirt I'm wearing. It's a soft cotton, my nipples poking through the material.

"Urgh," I groan. Bode smiles up at me before his teeth nip at the diamond hard tips. "Gah!"

He laves my nipples with attention. I'm dripping with need. Bode shifts, my hips cradling his in my own. His hands push my t-shirt up and over my head.

Greedy eyes take in my chest. "Do you know how sexy you are? How much I want you?"

"I can tell."

"You know what I really want?" Bode asks.

"What?"

"To eat your pussy."

I smile up at him. "I want that too."

"Good." He flips onto his back, pulling me with him. "Now, sit on my face."

Shucking off my shorts and underwear, I toss them to the side. I take my time moving up Bode's sexy body. I kiss and lick his abs. Nibble on his pecs. Groans and murmured *fucks* greet my ears.

I grind my hips over him, letting me feel exactly what he does to me. "You ready for me?"

"Fuck yes, Stevie." Bode slaps my ass and lifts me so my pussy is over his mouth. "I want you to come on my tongue."

He wastes no time as his tongue slides through my wet folds.

"Gah!" I hold tight to the headboard as his fingers dig into my ass, moving me over his mouth.

He licks and savors as I stare down at him. Bode doesn't take his eyes off me. A finger pushes inside me and it has my pleasure ramping up.

I grind my hips down over his mouth. Wanting more. No, *needing* more. Needing everything this man will give me.

The hand on my ass gives me another slap. It's Bode's

way of telling me he's ready for me to come. It's all I need to topple over the edge.

"Bode!" I shout. Heat floods my veins as my orgasm washes over me. His hands hold me up as I chase the high that always comes when I'm with Bode.

Sliding down his body, I collapse onto the bed. But he doesn't let me get far. His cock is sticking straight out and I want more.

"You want this?" He gives himself a lazy stroke.

I cover his hand with mine. "You know I do."

"You better be ready, Stevie. We're going to be doing this all night long."

"Yes."

With Bode traveling, it's going to be a long few weeks. I'll miss being able to connect with him like this.

Flipping me onto my back, he drags his cock through my wet folds. "I love how wet you get, baby."

"Only for you."

Bode clasps my chin and turns my head to kiss him as he pushes inside of me. He swallows my gasps and moans as he pumps his hips in and out of me.

"God, I love the way you take my cock. Squeezing it, like you want every fucking drop of my cum that I'll give you. So fucking good, Stevie."

I love the dirty talk. My pussy pulses around him. I'm already close to coming again, but I don't want to. I want Bode to come with me.

"I want you to come inside me. I need it, Bode."

"Hold on."

Linking his hands with mine, he puts them on the headboard. I tighten my grip as he jacks his hips inside of me.

One hand slips around me and finds my clit. He strums it to perfection.

"Bode. Oh, god!"

"That's it."

He moves faster and faster, his fingers moving in time. I know he's close. Squeezing his cock with every thrust inside, I try to take him over the edge with me, but he keeps going.

Damn this man and his stamina.

"So close, Stevie." Bode peppers my shoulder with kisses, nipping the soft skin there. "I want you to come for me so I can fucking unload inside of you."

I can't string two words together at his words as his moves slow. Each move inside of me gets me right where he wants me—at the edge of the cliff ready to erupt.

"C'mon, Stevie."

His fingers dig into my hips as his back covers mine.

One more pinch of my clit and I explode. My vision blacks as a kaleidoscope of colors explode against my eyelids.

The pleasure is so great, I almost miss Bode coming inside of me.

"Fuck yes!" He growls out.

Hard fingers mark my skin as he continues moving through his release. I will never get over the feeling of his release inside of me.

When he pulls out, my thighs are sticky.

"Fuck." He swipes a finger through my folds, bringing it to his lips. "We taste so fucking good together."

Flipping onto my back, I press up and clasp my fingers behind his neck to kiss him. Our chests brush, heartbeats syncing as we slowly come back down to earth.

Bode slows the kiss, dropping his forehead against mine. "I love you, Stevie."

"Not as much as I love you."

"I don't think that's possible." He smiles at me.

"Mmm. I think you might need to show me just how much you do love me."

And he does.

All night long.

And want to find out what happens after Dax and Chloe leave her wedding?! Preorder Breakaway now…Coming September 5, 2025!

Acknowledgments

Book number....TWENTY-SIX is out in the world!!

That one took me a minute to count to. Because it seems like I only started writing yesterday! This was the first time I tackled a surprise baby and I found I LOVED it! I mean, sassy grandmas moving in to help raise a baby? Say less! I fell in love with this little family and hope you did too! And thank you to my little book family I've created...Tina, Lily, Swati, Maria, Carrie, Claire...I love you all more than you know!

Thank you to every person that has read, reviewed, shared, created edits, TikToked...you name it, your support has been the best part of this journey! I love my readers more than anything! To my Street & Influencer Teams...your excitement for my books always puts a smile on my face! And to the Silver Society...thank you for making our little corner of the internet the best!

And to all the readers...I hope you're loving this team as much as I am! Your support means the world to me!

<3 Emily

Also by Emily Silver

Colorado Black Diamonds Hockey

Best Kept Secret

Best Laid Plans

Best of the Best

Best of Both Worlds

Nashville Knights

Game Misconduct

The Playmaker

Breakaway - coming September 5, 2025

Bar Down - coming October 24, 2025

Dixon Creek Ranch

Yours to Take

Yours to Hold

Yours to Be

Yours to Forget

Yours To Lose

Yours To Love

The Denver Mountain Lions

Roughing The Kicker

Pass Interference

Sideline Infraction

Illegal Contact

The Big Game

Moose Falls, Maine

Merry in Moose Falls

A Grump in Moose Falls - coming November 7, 2025

Standalones

Off the Deep End

The Highland Escape

Power Pose

Love Pucked - a sapphic hockey romance, coming October 10, 2025

The Ainsworth Royals

Royal Reckoning

Reckless Royal

Royal Relations

Royal Roots

The Love Abroad Series

An Icy Infatuation

A French Fling

A Sydney Surprise

Scan the QR code to read my books now!

About the Author

After winning a Young Author's Award in second grade, Emily Silver was destined to be a writer. She loves writing inclusive stories, with strong heroines and the swoony men who fall for them.

A lover of all things romance, Emily started writing books set in her favorite places around the world. As an avid traveler, she's been to all seven continents and sailed around the globe.

When she's not writing, Emily can be found sipping cocktails on her porch, reading all the romance she can get her hands on and planning her next big adventure!

Find her on social media to stay up to date on all her adventures and upcoming releases!

www.ingramcontent.com/pod-product-compliance
Lightning Source LLC
Chambersburg PA
CBHW020737310726

48969CB00002B/301